Second Edition Death

Elizabeth Penney

Annie's®
AnniesFiction.com

Library of Congress-in-Publication Data
Second Edition Death/ by Elizabeth Penney
p. cm.
I. Title
                        2017951012

AnniesFiction.com
(800) 282-6643
Secrets of the Castleton Manor Library™
Series Creator: Shari Lohner
Series Editor: Jane Haertel
Cover Illustrator: Jesse Reisch

10 11 12 13 14 | Printed in China | 9 8 7 6 5 4 3 2 1

"No, Watson, you can't go with me." Faith Newberry grabbed her down parka off the peg and put it on. "It's too cold out there." Lighthouse Bay on Cape Cod, Massachusetts, was usually fairly temperate as New England weather went. But not this year. Winter still had a firm grip on the countryside, even though it was early spring.

From his position in the hall, the tuxedo cat merely blinked. Faith knew from experience he was telling her that, while he wouldn't argue, his opinion was unchanged. He bided his time as she slipped on duck boots and tugged a knitted hat, a gift from her aunt Eileen, down over her ears. Only when she opened the door did he spring, becoming a black-and-white streak and disappearing.

Faith stepped out of the cottage and locked the door. If Watson had any sense, he'd follow her to Castleton Manor, where it was warm and toasty. Otherwise he'd have a long, cold wait until she came back. His poor little paws would be frozen.

Faith picked her way along the slushy path, her breath white in the frosty air. Despite the knobby treads on her boots, she had to be careful not to slip.

I wonder what on earth Marlene wants.

Marlene Russell, assistant manager at Castleton Manor where Faith worked as librarian and archivist, had awakened her with a call at dawn. Although the manor was closed this week to be refurbished and deep-cleaned, Marlene had informed Faith that her presence was urgently required. As usual, she wouldn't say why. Marlene was maddening like that.

So, instead of enjoying a well-deserved morning reading in front of the fire, Faith was headed to a meeting with her boss. *With any luck, a short one. I'll be free for the rest of the day, and Watson won't turn into an ice cube.*

Faith looked up at the manor and, as always, caught her breath at the sight. She didn't think she'd ever get over the beauty and majesty of the place. The magnificent French Renaissance structure sat like a palace in acres of elegantly groomed grounds. The rising sun glinted off three stories of windows, making it appear that the manor shone with welcoming light. Even now, exotic evergreens, shaped topiary, and a maze provided visual interest. Here and there statues stood, some in fountains currently dormant.

Faith skirted a stone woman holding an empty jug and took the path to the front door. This route led her past the terrace by the library, where through the French doors she spotted the two lamps she kept burning. She also spotted something else.

Watson sat close to one of the doors, his face almost pressed to the glass. She swore he was smiling. His expression clearly said, "What took you so long?"

"Rumpy, you little rascal," she called, shaking her finger at him. "How did you do that?" Rumpy was her pet name for him, bestowed due to the loss of most of his tail as a kitten. He'd been that way when she'd found him outside her Boston apartment years ago.

Farther along the front was the main entrance, and Faith entered there. She passed through the vestibule and reached the main hall, where furniture and rugs had been removed. Faith remembered hearing that the marble floors were scheduled to receive a good cleaning and polishing.

Inside the lobby, a clerk was behind the desk area organizing files, her casual T-shirt and jeans signaling that the place was closed. She gave Faith a friendly wave. "What are you doing here?"

"Meeting with Marlene," Faith said.

The young woman nodded sagely. "Enough said. Have a good day." She ducked down behind the counter.

Faith went past the grand staircase and through the banquet hall, then descended the stairs to the lower regions. The kitchen, laundry, and offices were in the so-called basement, although the high ceilings gave the area a pleasant atmosphere. Marlene's office was at the end of a corridor, near those used by other managers such as the executive chef and the head of housekeeping.

The door was slightly open, but Faith knocked anyway.

"Come in," Marlene called. As Faith entered, the manager eyed her from head to toe, twitching her pointed nose. She rose, smoothing her cashmere sweater over slim hips. Even during this casual time, Marlene dressed as if it was a normal workday. "Don't you hate the way down makes you look fat?"

Faith bit back the first reply that sprang to her lips. For Marlene, such a remark represented her effort at "girl talk," something Marlene hadn't mastered. She wore a stony, abrasive style like a suit of armor. Faith was grateful for any chink, hoping to eventually forge a real relationship. Until then, her skills in diplomacy were tested during every interaction. "It's freezing," she said. "Is it ever going to feel like spring?"

Marlene gestured for Faith to sit, then sat down, frowning. "Of course it is."

Faith shrugged out of her coat. "You wanted to meet?" Hopefully they could cut to the chase, she could collect Watson, and she and her cat could be back at the cottage within the hour.

The manager cocked her head, continuing to study Faith. "I have an assignment for you."

There went her plans. "I thought you weren't doing anything in the library except shampooing rugs."

"We aren't. This is an off-site project." Marlene folded her hands.

Do I have to pry it out of her? Patience. "That sounds . . . interesting. Where is it and what is it?" To her relief, she sounded neutral, not annoyed.

"Mr. Jaxon wants to lend your librarian services to a friend of his." Wolfe Jaxon and his mother, Charlotte, owned Castleton Manor. "Ava

Winterbourne is one of the project leaders for the upcoming Gothic Studies conference."

"She needs help planning the retreat?" Faith guessed. Her duties sometimes included collecting information and editions of books to supplement retreat activities. Faith also gave tours and occasionally lectures, and she prepared a display in the library representing whatever genre or author was being featured at the event. The display was already done for the conference, so she could enjoy her free week. Or so she'd thought.

Marlene waved a hand. "Something like that. She's writing a book and can use some assistance with research. The planning group is gathering at her home this week, and they want you there. To stay."

"Where's the house? London? Paris?" Faith attempted a joke.

"Don't be ridiculous. Right here in Lighthouse Bay. A house called Wintersea."

"Ah, Ava Winterbourne, Wintersea. I get it."

"It belongs to her husband's family. She's a newcomer." Marlene's lip curled as she slid back in her rolling chair. "I need to get back to work. You'll be reporting at Wintersea tomorrow morning. Eight o'clock sharp. Any further questions, ask Mrs. Winterbourne." She handed Faith a piece of paper with a phone number on it.

Yes ma'am. Faith took the slip of paper. "Thanks, Marlene. I'm sure it'll be a great experience." She forced herself to give the manager a smile.

Marlene observed her with a skeptical expression. Faith could practically read her mind. *If you think it'll be fun, maybe I need to talk Mr. Jaxon out of it.*

Faith plucked her coat off the chair and made for the door before Marlene could change her mind and give her another assignment, like dusting each and every one of Castleton's thousands of books.

The door nudged open a hair wider, and a familiar figure padded in. Watson. To Faith's horror, he wiggled his haunches and leaped, landing right in the middle of Marlene's desk.

Marlene jumped up with a scream, sending her chair backward on its wheels. It crashed into the credenza behind the desk, and several piles of papers slid to the floor.

Faith didn't know what to take care of first—the cat, her quaking boss, or the mess on the floor. The manor allowed pets on the premises. Not for the first time, Faith wondered why a woman who appeared to despise animals worked here.

Apparently oblivious to the disaster he had caused, Watson investigated the top of the desk, sniffing at the computer keyboard, a vase of flowers, and a framed photograph of Castleton Manor.

Marlene finally found her voice. She pointed with a shaking finger. "Get that creature out of my office."

Watson leveled her a look as if to say, "Who are you calling a creature?" Before Faith could reach him, he hopped down and sauntered toward the door.

Faith lurched into action. "I'm so sorry. Let me pick up those papers." She hunkered down and gathered them in both hands. "I don't know what got into him. You know he's usually very well-behaved."

Marlene gave one of her trademark sniffs. "Depends on what you call well-behaved, I guess." She pushed her chair out of the way so Faith could reach the rest of the papers.

Faith stared up at Marlene, realization dawning. "You know what? Watson likes you. That's why he tries to get under your skin." Standing, she attempted to arrange the retrieved paperwork in some semblance of order.

"Leave that. I'll handle it." Marlene's tone brooked no argument. "Are you ready for the Gothic Studies conference?"

Faith had thought so, but now a seed of doubt sprouted. "I'll double-check."

"You do that. Now I really need to get back to work." She sat and pulled her chair up to the desk.

Thus dismissed, Faith didn't wait around to receive more orders or criticism. "Have a good day." At her boss's grunted reply, she threw a look over her shoulder. To her surprise, a tiny smile played around Marlene's lips. Watson had made another conquest.

Upstairs on her way to the library, Faith skirted the team setting up to polish the marble floor in the gallery. Even the statue of Agatha Christie was getting a scrubbing. The place was going to be gleaming and gorgeous when they reopened.

Faith unlocked the library door and stepped into the paper- and leather-scented hush. After months of working here, she still felt her heart lift every time she saw the magnificent room with its two stories of fully lined bookshelves, acres of carved woodwork, and gigantic fireplace. She paused to inhale the atmosphere and then crossed to the display of Gothic literature she had put together.

While many thought the Gothic genre consisted of authors like Phyllis A. Whitney, Victoria Holt, and Barbara Michaels, its origins were much earlier. Thanks to Castleton Manor's exquisite and valuable collection, Faith had found early editions of *The Castle of Otranto*, the first Gothic novel; *The Mysteries of Udolpho*, the first female-written Gothic; and "The Vampyre," a short story by a little-known contemporary of Lord Byron named John Polidori, who had also served as Byron's physician. She'd even included Jane Austen's send-up of the genre, *Northanger Abbey*.

Another shelf held the Brontë sisters, *Frankenstein* by Mary Shelley, and Daphne du Maurier's classic *Rebecca*. And for fun, Faith had gathered first editions of the twentieth-century Gothic romances that many read and loved. She hoped the guests would enjoy the range and breadth of books she'd put together.

A loud meow caught her attention, and she glanced around, trying to spot the cat in the dim room. He was on the balcony, staring down at her. "Watson, how did you get up there?" His ability to disappear only to reappear in unexpected places never failed to amaze her. "Come on. I'm going home for a second breakfast."

As she'd hoped, that brought him running. By the time she reached the library door, he was twining through her legs, almost making her trip. "You're always underfoot, Rumpy," she scolded. "What am I going to do with you?"

A thought struck. *What am I going to do with him? I can't leave him alone for an entire week.*

After an otherwise relaxing day at home, Faith was no closer to an answer about what to do with Watson while she was away. Her first choice, veterinarian Midge Foster, was going to a conference. She'd tried calling her aunt Eileen but only got voice mail. Brooke Milner, the sous-chef at Castleton Manor, didn't answer her phone either. Fortunately there was a Candle House Book Club meeting tonight, and she could corner her friends there.

"We've been lucky," she told her pet as she washed the supper dishes. "I've never had to put you in a kennel."

An expression passed across Watson's face that could only be regarded as a sneer. He seemed to say, "Kennel? Isn't that for dogs?"

Faith laughed. "Boarding facility, I mean. Anyway, I haven't had a chance to find a good cat sitter for you yet." She preferred to have someone stay so Watson could come and go at his leisure. She wiped the last of the dishes and put them in the cupboard. "Do you want to tag along with me tonight?"

The book club was as pet friendly as Castleton Manor, due in large part to Midge. In addition to her practice in town, Midge provided a concierge service to the manor. The versatile vet also owned Happy Tails Gourmet Bakery, where she sold scrumptious delicacies for pets, such as shrimp whiskers and Watson's favorite, tunaroons.

Watson's answer was to run to the door.

Faith bundled up again, grumbling at the annoyance of wearing boots, a parka, a hat, and gloves. *Oh, for the days of summer when I can go outside in shorts and a T-shirt!* They got into her Honda CR-V, and Watson took his preferred spot in the passenger seat.

The village of Lighthouse Bay wasn't far away, too short a distance for the vehicle to warm up. Faith sat shivering as she drove, eager to get to the Candle House Library, where the meetings were held. Then she remembered Wintersea, her destination in the morning. *There's time before the meeting. Might as well find it now.* She had already looked it up online because she didn't want to get lost and arrive late.

A wall appeared on her left, and she recognized it from the website images as belonging to Wintersea. She'd noticed this property, of course, but she'd never seen the house, hidden behind a thick band of trees. Faith slowed to a crawl, seeking the entrance. There it was, a wide iron gate. She halted the vehicle and rolled down the window, trying to get a glimpse of the mansion through the scrollwork.

Nothing. Not a single light could be seen from here. The place appeared deserted. Then she spotted a very small sign on the right-hand pillar, obscured by a tangle of dead vines. It read *Wintersea* in faded script. The wind kicked up, and the vines swayed, giving the scene an eerie aspect.

Faith hastily rolled up her window and drove on, a knot of excitement forming in her belly. Curious by nature, she looked forward to seeing inside the old mansion. According to the Internet, it had been built around 1840.

She reached the library with five minutes to spare before the meeting started. Usually she stopped at Snickerdoodles Bakery & Tea Shop next door, but today she didn't have time. With any luck, one of the others would have brought provisions.

Faith wheeled into a spot next to her aunt's ruby-red Mustang Coupe, shut off the engine, and hopped out. She and Watson hurried up the walk to the historic stone building, a former candle factory now home to a cozy and welcoming library.

Eileen, Brooke, and Midge were seated in front of the huge fireplace with a young woman Faith didn't recognize. The woman was very pretty, with huge dark eyes, a cascade of dark curls, and creamy skin. Everyone held mugs of coffee and munched on treats.

Atticus, Midge's Chihuahua, trotted over to sniff at Watson.

Watson simply glared.

"Be nice," Faith scolded.

"Faith, I'm so glad you made it," Eileen said with a warm smile. "I'm sorry I didn't call you back. I was out of town all day." She put a hand on the newcomer's arm. "Ava, this is my niece Faith Newberry. Faith, this is Ava Winterbourne."

Faith paused in the act of unzipping her parka. "Ava Winterbourne? The owner of Wintersea?"

The other woman looked surprised. "And you're the librarian at Castleton Manor?"

Eileen appeared puzzled, Midge snorted, and Brooke asked, "You two know each other?"

"Not yet," Faith explained. "I'm going to be a resource to Ava this week at a meeting. I just found out this morning."

"The planning committee for the Gothic Studies conference is gathering at my house," Ava said. "We're doing some work of our own as well as going over the retreat schedule again. Faith will be our research librarian."

"So that's what your meeting with Marlene was about," Brooke said.

Faith had mentioned the impromptu assignment in an earlier text message to Brooke without telling her the details.

Faith merely smiled and nodded, not wanting Ava to think she was less than thrilled about working with her. She joined the others, stopping to grab a cup of coffee and a couple of pumpkin cookies on the way.

"You'll love Wintersea," Eileen said. "It's gorgeous. Gothic Revival, isn't that right, Ava?"

Ava gave a husky laugh. "It is indeed. I tell people I married my husband for his house. It's the perfect place for me to live, since I study Gothic literature."

"She's working on a book." Midge snapped her fingers at her dog. "Atticus, come to Mama and quit plaguing that cat."

Atticus, who had been trailing Watson like a second tail, veered off and ran toward his mistress.

"Publish or perish," Ava said, rolling her eyes. "It's my doctoral dissertation. 'Ruins and Romance: The Symbolism of Setting in Gothic Literature.'"

"Sounds fascinating," Faith said earnestly.

Ava chuckled. "Thank you. I'm still working on the title. It's more interesting than it sounds." She picked up her handbag and began to forage. "I brought those photographs of Irish castles I mentioned, Eileen. The ones you wanted to see." Ava looked bewildered as she searched, her movements increasingly frenzied. She pulled out items—a wallet, a hairbrush, pens, a pack of tissues, a small notebook. A tube of lipstick hit the floor and rolled away.

"I know I put that envelope in my purse," Ava said, her tone frantic. "I remember doing it this afternoon. Or do I?" Her face crumpled, and she burst into tears. "I'm losing my mind."

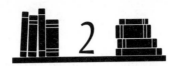

2

The women stared at Ava.

Eileen picked up the package of tissues and took one out. "It's okay. We all have meltdowns now and then." She handed the tissue to Ava, who accepted it gratefully.

"You should have seen me when I was finishing vet school," Midge said. "I was a mess. You'd think you'd relax when you see the light at the end of the tunnel, but instead the pressure intensifies."

Brooke and Faith gathered Ava's possessions from the floor, pulling the hairbrush away from a curious Atticus, who sniffed at it. Faith found the lipstick resting under Watson's paw.

Ava dabbed at her eyes. "You're all so nice. But it's not my dissertation. I really think I'm losing my mind." Crumpling the tissue in her hand, she gazed around at each face. "Strange things have been happening. You'd probably think I'm crazy if I told you about them."

"No, we wouldn't," Brooke said. "Believe me, lots of unusual incidents happen in Lighthouse Bay. Ask Faith."

"What do you mean?" With a sniff, Ava raised the tissue and wiped her nose.

Faith shrugged. "We've had to solve a few mysteries around here, that's all. And somehow I seem to end up in the middle of them."

Ava's chest rose and fell with a huge breath, as if she were releasing a giant burden. "All right, I'll tell you. But promise not to make fun of me. You might want to get more coffee. It's a long story."

The ladies got up and refilled their cups and grabbed cookies, then sat, ready to listen.

Ava sipped at her drink, apparently gathering her thoughts. "Can anything be successful when it's built upon a tragedy?" she asked rhetorically, her lips twisting in a grimace. "It's a question I ask myself. You see, I'm Winslow's second wife. We've been married almost a year." She paused. "Regina, his first wife, committed suicide two and a half years ago."

"I remember that," Eileen said. "It was so tragic. She jumped off the outlook tower at Wintersea onto the rocks below. Depression, they said."

"Regina was a writer, right?" Midge asked. "I heard she had published a couple of books."

"She had. Mystery novels." Ava took up the tale again. "We were actually friends in college, but we lost touch. I don't know if you're aware of this, but Winslow runs a small publishing house, Winterbourne Press. He specializes in nonfiction, mostly history and literary analysis. A few years ago, I ran into Regina and Winslow at a conference. I was heartbroken when she died. She was so beautiful and vibrant and smart." She blinked rapidly, tears welling.

The others remained silent, allowing her to regroup.

"When I approached Winslow about publishing my dissertation—if it's ever done—we bonded over our loss. Then one thing led to another, and here we are." She shrugged helplessly.

"You mustn't feel guilty," Eileen said. "I'm sure Regina would want Winslow to be happy."

Faith wondered if Ava did feel guilty about marrying Winslow and that was preying on her mind. Maybe she felt she didn't deserve happiness after stepping into her friend's place.

Watson, always one to sense distress, padded over to Ava and leaped into her lap.

Ava laughed in delight as she rubbed the cat's chin. "You're probably right. It's what Winslow always says." Her tone grew somber. "Winslow was absolutely crushed when it happened. Our friends told me they were worried about him for a while." She picked up Watson and nuzzled his head with her cheek. He tolerated the caress politely.

"They told me he was quite transformed when we fell in love. He became a new man."

Brooke sighed in satisfaction. "That's wonderful. Healed by true love." She was a romantic, and happily ever after was her favorite story line.

"I hope so." Ava released a squirming Watson onto the floor. He liked affection but only so much of it. "It's not only that Regina died. It's *where* she died. You see, Winslow's grandmother was murdered in that tower back in the 1930s."

"Why, bless his heart, that's terrible!" When Midge got upset, her Southern roots showed.

"Winslow hadn't been born yet, of course, but it certainly affected his father. He was only a baby when it happened." Ava gave a tiny smile. "If you haven't guessed, Winslow is quite a bit older than me."

"I hate to be nosy," Brooke said, "but what *did* happen to his grandmother?"

Faith silently thanked her friend for her bluntness, since she was curious too.

"Violet Winterbourne was found strangled on the top floor. The handyman they believe did it fell to his death while trying to escape down to the beach. A really valuable figurine also disappeared that night—a Meissen statue of Cupid. The theory is that Violet interrupted him while he was stealing it in an act of revenge. She'd fired him the day before. Violet had a private sitting room in the tower, where she kept her porcelain collection."

"Did they ever find the figurine?" Eileen asked.

Ava shook her head. "It probably ended up smashed on the rocks and washed away by the tide."

"This is very interesting, sugar," Midge said in her soft drawl, "but you haven't told us why it's upsetting you so." She tapped her temple. "Causing you to question your own sanity."

The young woman shifted in her chair, the uncomfortable look on her face conveying that she regretted bringing up the topic.

"It's all right, Ava," Eileen said. "You're among friends."

Ava laughed nervously. "It's not that. You know how something seems upsetting, but when you try to talk about it, it seems stupid?"

"We've all been there," Brooke said. "So don't worry. We won't laugh."

There was a pause. "I keep misplacing things," she finally said in little more than a whisper. "Then they show up later in places I don't remember going."

Eileen shot a look of concern at Faith and the others. But her voice was calm when she said, "Been there too. Go on."

"Maybe that's my fault, me being distracted with all the work for my dissertation, right? But I'm also hearing things. At night, mostly." Fear flashed across Ava's pretty features. "Footsteps at night. Whispering voices in the walls. Either I'm crazy from stress or Wintersea is haunted."

Alarm trilled in Faith's mind. Her seemingly simple assignment had suddenly become more complicated. She didn't believe in ghosts, so either Ava *was* imagining things—which didn't speak well of her state of mind—or there was another explanation.

Eileen maintained her serene demeanor. "That's why it's fortunate Faith will be staying with you for a week. She'll get to the bottom of it."

Ava turned to Faith, eyes filled with hope. "It will help just to have you there. I'm sure of it."

I'm not. Faith pushed down her doubts, saying only, "I'll do my best." Watson reappeared, rubbing against her legs, and she reached down to run a hand along his back. "That reminds me. I need a cat sitter. Does anyone know one?"

"You can bring Watson with you," Ava said. "In fact, please do. It will be nice to have him around."

Watson looked up at Faith, and she swore she saw triumph gleaming in his eyes. He wanted to go to Wintersea. *Well, that makes one of us!*

"Thanks, Ava. I appreciate your offer," Faith said. "He won't be any trouble, I promise."

Eileen nodded. "I'm glad that's settled. Shall we discuss our book?"

She held up the latest in a charming antique shop mystery series.

"I loved it," Ava said. "So refreshingly different from my usual dark reading. And guess what, Watson? There's a cat in it."

He gazed at her as if to say, "I know. What self-respecting mystery doesn't feature a cat?"

As the women discussed the book, the mood lightened. Even Ava seemed less anxious, her laughter ringing out frequently.

After they adjourned, Faith quickly gathered her things and picked up Watson. "I need to get home and start packing," she told the others.

They all called farewells.

Ava said, "See you tomorrow. How's ten o'clock?"

Much better than Marlene's early-morning summons. "That sounds fine. See you then."

Faith pushed through the door into the night air, which was even colder than when she arrived. "Let's hurry home, Watson." Grimacing when an icy wind blasted her face, Faith moved along the sidewalk as fast as possible.

At her SUV, she pressed the fob to unlock the doors, then got behind the wheel.

Watson wriggled out of her grasp and climbed into the passenger seat.

As Faith wound along the familiar route to her cottage, she wondered about her upcoming stay at Wintersea.

Either her hostess had an overactive imagination or there was something very peculiar going on. If it was the latter, Faith had the feeling she'd soon be in it up to her eyeballs.

At least she'd have her cat to keep her company.

3

The tall iron gate at Wintersea was open when Faith arrived the next morning. With a thrill of anticipation, she turned onto the paved drive and entered the estate. Dense woods crowded the road, skeletal trees looming out of the fog that covered the ground. Under her wheels, slush splashed, making the going slow and treacherous along the winding road.

"I hope we live to get there," she told Watson as she navigated a particularly bad corner bordered by a huge oak. Judging by the scarred bark, she wasn't the only one who'd had difficulty rounding the curve.

The tense driving made her arrival at the house especially sweet. As she emerged from the woods, Wintersea appeared. Beyond the house was a glimpse of the ocean, promising spectacular views from the interior.

Faith instinctively slowed to a crawl as she took in the mansion. Dark gray with a red slate roof, the main house with its pointed front gables was bracketed by two turrets, one slender and the other wide. Lacy trim adorned the gables above diamond-paned windows. It was gorgeous and, as Ava had noted, very Gothic in style.

She drove around the circular driveway and parked in front of the entrance. After shutting off the engine, she sat for a minute, half-expecting someone to come out and greet her. But there was no movement in the house, and all was still and silent. The place seemed deserted. The raucous cawing of a crow startled her as it flapped across the garden toward the woods.

"Let's do it, Watson," she said, taking a deep breath. Faith left her keys in the ignition, not sure if Ava would want her to move the vehicle. Scooping up her handbag and Watson, she climbed the short flight of stairs to the front door, which was arched like the windows. She rang the bell, hearing it chime inside.

Nothing.

She rang again. As she considered giving Ava a call, the door swung open.

A tall woman wearing a black pantsuit stood there, glaring down her long nose at Faith. She wore her dark hair scraped back into a bun, and her skin was pale, untouched by blush or lipstick. "May I help you?" she intoned in a deep voice, her expression conveying quite clearly that she hoped the answer was no.

"I'm Faith Newberry. The librarian?" To Faith's horror, she found her voice rising in a question. She cleared her throat and tried again. "Ava is expecting me."

The woman cocked a brow. "Mrs. Winterbourne is busy, but please do come in." She stood back barely far enough for Faith to step inside. "What is that cat doing here?"

"This is Watson. Ava specifically requested that I bring him."

To her relief, the woman didn't argue. "Very good, ma'am." She shut the heavy door firmly. "Do you have additional luggage?"

Faith nodded.

"Harrison will fetch it and park your car." She held out her hand. "Keys?"

"They're in the ignition. I left them there in case I needed to move it." Faith felt a childish satisfaction at sharing this information. There was something about this woman that aroused her contrary side. "And I didn't catch your name."

"I'm Mrs. Danbury, the housekeeper. Come this way." She glided across the parquet floor to the staircase along the back wall.

Now that Faith was safely admitted into the home, she glanced around. The red wallpaper and dark woodwork, along with the paneled ceiling and the carved, heavy furniture, gave the place an oppressive air. Even her cottage, which could almost fit inside this hall, felt more open and airy—and welcoming.

One of the doors off the hall opened, and Ava popped out. "Welcome, Faith! We're working in the library if you'd like to join us. But please get settled in first."

Chatter and laughter drifted through the half-open door behind her, and Faith glimpsed movement.

"I'm glad to be here, Ava. Give me half an hour and I'll be down."

"Take good care of her, Mrs. Danbury." Ava went back into the library. "Our librarian is here," Faith heard her say before the heavy door closed again.

Mrs. Danbury began to climb the long flight of stairs, and Faith followed, carrying Watson. At the top, the corridor branched off in several directions, the oriental runner extending for what seemed like miles in each direction.

The housekeeper turned right and then left, Faith logging the route so she could find her way back downstairs later.

"Here we are." Mrs. Danbury removed a large ornate key from the key ring on her belt and unlocked the door. "This is one of the turret rooms. I hope you find it to your satisfaction."

Faith's breath caught as she stepped onto the thick Persian carpet. The room was furnished with massive furniture—a four-poster bed, wardrobe, and bureau—and the view from the window was stunning. The red velvet curtains were pulled wide to let in the day's meager light, and the ocean was a vast, silver expanse rippling under an ominous sky. The fog that had plagued Faith on her drive wound tendrils through statuesque groupings of specimen trees. Across the grounds, at the edge of the cliff, sat a squat stone tower with a conical roof. The top story was open to the air while slit windows revealed a bit of the rooms below.

Faith moved closer to the window, drawn in morbid fascination to the tower. *That's where Winslow's grandmother died. And where Regina killed herself.*

"There is an en suite bathroom," Mrs. Danbury said, opening a door.

Tiled in white, the bathroom had both a shower stall and a soaking tub. The towels were thick white terry, and baskets held soaps, shampoo, and bath salts.

"This is lovely," Faith said.

"Is there anything else, ma'am?" Mrs. Danbury asked.

"I'm fine. Thank you. Please do have, er, Harrison bring up my things."

"Right away, ma'am." The housekeeper bowed slightly from the waist in a jerky movement, then slipped away in her gliding gait.

Watson meowed.

She set him on the floor. "Come explore our new digs."

The cat walked slowly, turning his head to get the lay of the land. Then he started exploring, sniffing the bed legs, the door, and the rest of the furniture. He seemed especially interested in a dull tapestry depicting a castle scene hanging on one wall.

A knock sounded on the door, and Faith answered. Then she took a step back in shock.

An enormous man with a huge scar running down the side of his face stood there. Coupled with his crew cut, lantern jaw, and protruding brow, he resembled a character in a horror film.

Realizing she was staring, Faith tore her gaze away from his face. "You must be Harrison. I'm Faith. Thanks for delivering my things."

The man gave her a brusque nod and stepped inside to set her possessions on the carpet. "Is there anything else, ma'am?" His voice was a whisper.

"No, I'm all set." Faith noticed she was whispering back.

With a nod, he turned on his heels and left, his footsteps as quiet as his voice.

Faith shut the bedroom door and began unpacking. She laid a nightgown and robe on the bed and put her toiletry kit in the bathroom. The house was luxurious, no question. There was even a wall-mounted hair dryer and a ceiling heater. Her coat and work outfits went in the wardrobe, and her jeans, tops, and undergarments went in the bureau.

She was shutting the top bureau drawer when movement in the mirror caught her eye. The tapestry hanging on the wall was swaying. With an intake of air, she whirled around. *What is causing that? The windows aren't open.*

Mrs. Danbury pushed aside the tapestry and walked into the room, holding a vase of lovely flowers—irises, white roses, and sweet peas. She stopped short when she saw Faith. "I'm sorry, ma'am. I thought you were downstairs already."

Faith let out her breath. "I didn't know there was a door back there."

Mrs. Danbury set the vase on a table near the window. "There is indeed. It leads to the service area." She gave the vase a half turn and nodded, apparently satisfied.

"I will be going down in a minute," Faith said. "Thank you for the flowers."

The woman gave the bed skirt a last tug and plumped a pillow. "I hope everything will be satisfactory, ma'am." Then she left, taking the exit behind the tapestry.

Faith collapsed on the bed, her thoughts racing. On the face of it, it was entirely innocent for the housekeeper to bring her flowers. They were gorgeous and must have cost a fortune. But why had she come up the back stairs? So no one would know she was in here?

Don't be silly. The staff at Castleton Manor use the servants' passages all the time. It must be something about this particular housekeeper that had her on edge.

Watson jumped up beside her, and she ran her hand along his back, then allowed him to butt her hand with his head. "Oh, Rumpy, I'm probably imagining things. But this house and Ava's staff *are* a little creepy." She laughed. "Listen to me. I'm as skittish as a heroine in a Gothic novel."

She told herself to stop being ridiculous and went to join Ava and the others.

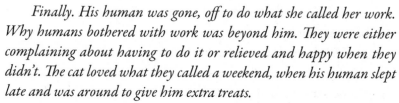

Finally. His human was gone, off to do what she called her work. Why humans bothered with work was beyond him. They were either complaining about having to do it or relieved and happy when they didn't. The cat loved what they called a weekend, when his human slept late and was around to give him extra treats.

Everyone should be a cat. Cats knew how to live. Eat, sleep, cuddle, and explore. That reminded him. Why was he dawdling? He hopped off the bed where he'd been feigning a nap.

The heavy tapestry posed a bit of a challenge, but he finally nudged it aside with his nose, followed by a paw. Aha! As he'd thought, the door was ajar, wide enough for him to slip out onto the staircase. The human—the dark, severe one—had not quite closed it.

The cat sniffed the air, testing it for intriguing odors. From below drifted the savory smell of roasting chicken, always a temptation.

But above . . . that held secrets.

4

The library door was shut so Faith knocked, feeling somewhat intrusive. She still wasn't sure what her role was at Wintersea, and she didn't want to overstep or underperform. She hoped Ava could clarify her tasks soon.

A slender blonde with large blue eyes answered the door. She looked Faith up and down as though she were examining something distasteful. "Yes?"

Who is she, Marlene the second? Trying her best not to be rattled by the woman, Faith said, "I'm Faith Newberry, the librarian. Here at Ava Winterbourne's request."

"Oh. Come in." The woman stepped back. "I'm Stephanie Schilling, Winslow's assistant."

"Nice to meet you." Faith entered the library, noticing first the floor-to-ceiling bookcases lining the walls. Between the bookcases, deep-set windows featured cushioned seats, and comfortable leather furniture was arranged around the room, right now being used by Ava's guests.

Ava rose from a wingback chair. "Everyone, this is Faith Newberry, the wonderful research librarian I stole from Castleton Manor for the week." She introduced Faith to the others.

A tiny woman with masses of wavy red hair was Dr. Cassandra Cooper. Dr. Roger Lewis was cadaverous and beaky, with a British accent. Dr. Sean O'Malley was tall and broad shouldered with an Irish brogue, twinkling blue eyes, and an infectious smile. The men wore tweed jackets. Cassandra and Ava were dressed in flowing skirts and lacy blouses. They all looked as if they'd stepped out of history.

"Have a seat, Faith," Ava said. She checked the mantel clock.

"Coffee should be arriving any moment."

Indeed, as Faith settled herself in a wing chair placed on the edge of the group, where she could watch and listen, a rattling of china was heard.

Harrison opened the library door, and Mrs. Danbury swept in, carrying a tray. The housekeeper deposited her burden on a low table and proceeded to fill and pass out cups. A plate of gingersnaps made the rounds. Faith accepted coffee and a cookie.

"Will there be anything else, ma'am?" Mrs. Danbury asked, brushing her hands across her apron.

"We're all set. Thank you," Ava said. "We'll have lunch at one."

Mrs. Danbury nodded and left the room, closing the door behind her.

In the hush left by her departure, the clank of spoons and murmurs of appreciation were heard.

"Your cook is fantastic." Sean reached for another cookie. "Can I steal her?"

Ava opened her mouth to speak, but Stephanie got there first. "Meg is wonderful, isn't she?" The assistant glanced at Ava. "She's been with Winslow for years. She's very loyal to him."

But not to Ava? Faith straightened in her chair. Obviously there were undercurrents here, and it would be wise to pay attention.

Ava's cheeks flushed. "Yes, she's an indispensable part of our household, as are Mrs. Danbury and Harrison." She slightly stressed the word *our*.

"Now that you've gorged on cookies, Sean, shall we return to our discussion about the conference?" Cassandra's tone was teasing, and Faith noticed that she watched the Irishman closely with a look of longing in her eyes.

Sean, who had been reaching for yet another gingersnap, pulled back his hand with a laugh. "I am being rather a pig, aren't I?" He leafed through the papers on his lap. "Where were we? Oh yes, which of us gets to give the opening keynote address at the conference." He grinned. "Which happens to come with a $1,000 stipend."

"I would think Winslow, as the sponsor, would want someone with a doctorate," Stephanie said. "Someone with the appropriate credentials."

Ava chewed on her bottom lip as though she wanted to speak but didn't dare. She didn't have her PhD yet, Faith recalled.

"Even though that would eliminate his wife?" Sean's eyes flashed. "Surely we should review everyone's proposals and choose the most interesting topic."

Roger cleared his throat. "That criterion is why you should select me. My paper on Victorian Gothic and its iteration in the steampunk genre is both timely and of interest to the younger crowd." His smile was thin. "We need to appeal to that generation, or our work will lose its relevance."

"And publishing deals." Cassandra's tone was wry. "As you all know, I'm writing a book about female Gothic authors. I should be the keynote. Women don't get the recognition they deserve as founders of Gothic literature. Where would it be without Ann Radcliffe or Mary Shelley?"

"In the capable hands of Edgar Allan Poe and Bram Stoker, I suppose," Roger said. His smug smile was infuriating. "You know the first Gothic was called *The Castle of Otranto*, and it was written by a man, Horace Walpole, in 1764."

"You're insufferable, Roger." Cassandra jumped up and stamped her tiny foot as dramatically as any Gothic heroine. "It was Clara Reeve who first balanced fantastical elements with eighteenth-century realism, broadening the genre's appeal and rescuing it from an early death after Walpole's book languished."

Roger bristled as though planning a counterattack, but then his gaze softened. He waved a hand. "I concede the battle to you, my dear. You have my vote for the keynote address."

Cassandra glowed with victory.

"You need the money more than I do," Roger added.

"What about me?" Sean asked before Cassandra could reply. "Irish

Gothic literature is woefully obscure, although Bram Stoker was Irish, as you know. I would enjoy the opportunity to share its wonders with our attendees." His lifted brow and mild tone of sarcasm revealed that he knew his wording was rather pompous.

Faith stifled a laugh. *Are they going to talk and act like characters out of the books they study this whole time?*

"Oh, of course, Sean." Cassandra's expression was apologetic. "You should do it." The fisted hands in her lap revealed her conflict.

She wants the prize badly but cares for Sean, Faith guessed.

Roger harrumphed. "I might agree, but I think it should go to someone with a book deal." He stood, hands clasped behind his back, and began to pace. "My latest tome is due out in May."

"Ah, you got me." Sean put a hand to his chest as though wounded. "Right where it counts—in the publishing credits."

"If you'd get your proposal to Winslow, you might have your deal," Ava said. "He told me he's been waiting for months."

Sean hung his head, faking contrition. "Duly noted. He'll have it after the conference."

"That's what you said last year," Ava said crisply. Then she clapped. "Let's get back to the conference agenda, shall we? If we get it done before lunch, we can have the afternoon free to work."

"Free to work. There's an oxymoron," Sean said.

Shifting in her seat, Cassandra asked briskly, "Where were we? Stephanie, do you know?"

The assistant had been a quiet observer, but now she leafed through papers with an officious air. "All the speakers are set, but someone mentioned rearranging the workshop order."

That remark sparked a tedious debate about which workshops to put together in the same track and which got the coveted midmorning slots. According to Sean, who was right in Faith's eyes, too early meant people either sleeping or lingering over breakfast, and after lunch was a lost cause. By two o'clock, everyone was pining for a change of scene.

The others had their own opinions, which they discussed at length.

What could be more long-winded than a planning group made up of professors? Faith surreptitiously reached into a nearby bookshelf and pulled out a copy of short stories. The first was "The Old Nurse's Story," written by Elizabeth Gaskell in 1852. Soon she was absorbed.

A while later, the sound of someone calling her name broke into her awareness. With a start, she looked up to see Ava standing over her. They were the only ones still in the library. Heat flashed up her neck at being caught not paying attention.

"I'm sorry." Faith set the book aside. "I only meant to glance through it."

Ava laughed. "I don't blame you. That was an extremely dull debate. I wanted you to know that lunch is ready." She led the way out of the room. "Afterward, we'll have quiet time and work on our projects. Perhaps you can gather reference books for us."

"I'd be happy to. Here or at Castleton?" As Faith entered the front hall, she spied Watson lurking behind a huge oriental vase that held umbrellas. He craned his neck slightly as though to say he was keeping an eye on her. Then she remembered she'd left the bedroom door shut. *How did he escape?*

Behind Ava's back, she shook her finger at him and frowned. She hadn't had a chance to ask Ava if he could roam free. There were many antiques at Wintersea, and some people were fussy about allowing animals to sit on them. Or scratch them, though fortunately Watson never did that.

No time like the present to ask about it, before he was spotted. "Ava, concerning my cat, would you prefer he stay in my room?"

"Oh no, he's a guest too. He can have full rein of the house. I don't mind." Ava jumped and squealed.

Faith looked down and saw Watson winding around her hostess's legs. "I guess he heard you. I'm not even sure how he got down here. Rumpy is a sneaky one."

Watson dashed on ahead, wiggling his bobbed tail.

"I see why you call him Rumpy. He's adorable." Ava ushered Faith through a doorway. "Here we are."

The dining room was easily one of the most unusual rooms Faith had ever seen. Panels of opalescent glass bricks were set in one wall, filtering the daylight through squares of light turquoise, pale coffee, and white.

At Faith's exclamation, Ava said, "That's Tiffany glass. Exquisite, isn't it? Check out the ceiling. Those are cork tiles. They're really unusual in a Gothic Revival home."

They joined the others gathered around a buffet table, where a tureen of soup and plates of sandwiches waited. The admirable Meg had prepared food worthy of a gourmet café, filling focaccia bread and crusty baguettes with roast beef, salmon, and turkey. The soup was clam chowder, with whole clams.

As Sean filled his soup bowl, he whispered to Faith, "The food is why I didn't argue about meeting here."

"I heard that," Stephanie said, sidling up beside the Irishman. She held a plate with a tiny pile of salad on it. "I thought it was my company that attracted you." Her eyes were brazenly flirtatious.

He dropped the ladle back into the soup tureen with a clank, his mouth opening and shutting.

Faith sympathized. It was often hard to find an appropriate response to a blatant attack like that.

Sean pulled at his collar. "Yes, of course, Stephanie. Seeing you is always a delight."

Good save. With a soft snort, Faith retrieved the ladle and filled a bowl, then grabbed her plate and headed for the empty chair between Roger and Cassandra. Watson was nowhere in sight, and Faith hoped he wasn't getting up to some mischief.

"Do you live locally?" Cassandra asked her.

Faith launched into an explanation of how she'd ended up at Castleton Manor, taking bites of lunch in between.

On her other side, Roger ate swiftly and silently, occasionally writing notes in a small notebook.

Cassandra noticed Faith glancing at him. "That's a true academic for you. The gears are always turning."

"Librarians are the same way," Faith said. "I'm always thinking about the book I just read or the one I want to read next."

"What book is that at the moment?" Roger asked, his focus still on his notebook.

Faith's mind went blank. Then she remembered the short stories. "I was reading a collection of famous Gothic firsts by women authors earlier today."

Cassandra laughed. "Glad to see you're in my camp, Faith."

Faith wasn't necessarily, but she didn't argue. She could already see that dealing with this group would require delicacy and tact. Their intelligent, analytical minds were quick to seize upon any nuance or implication, whether intended by the speaker or not.

A paw batted at her ankle, claws sheathed.

There he is. But why is he doing that? Nothing Watson did was random. She reached down to stroke his fur and felt something stuck on his back. A sticky note. Without reading it, she put it in her pocket to look at later.

She noticed Mrs. Danbury standing in front of the buffet table, checking the food. Where had she come from? Faith was facing the door, and surely she would have seen her entering the room.

"This may be a silly question," Faith said, "but how did the housekeeper get in here?"

Cassandra turned and pointed to the wood paneling, which appeared seamless to Faith's eyes. "There's a hidden door leading to the kitchen."

Seated nearby, Ava added, "The Winterbourne who built this place was a bit obsessive. Not only did he want unobtrusive service, but he wanted to disguise the doors leading to the service area. The effect is that the staff seem to appear and then disappear after performing their duties."

Castleton Manor also had a plethora of hidden doorways and passages. Had making servants invisible been the intent of the first Jaxon? She'd have to ask Wolfe when she saw him next.

After lunch, Roger and Cassandra took tables in the library to work. Watson scampered back upstairs for a nap, Faith assumed. Ava sat in the parlor next to the fire with her laptop, and Sean went out to the conservatory, which was heated to a tropical temperature to keep the palm trees and exotic plants alive. Faith made the rounds, taking requests and searching the library for the required volumes.

Sean glanced up as she brought him a book of Irish legends and myths. He was seated right under the sheltering fronds of a palm next to a red hibiscus. "I'm pretending I'm in the tropics," he said with a grin.

"If you had a drink with an umbrella, the illusion would be complete," Faith joked.

"Now there's an idea." He fanned himself dramatically. "If you see Mrs. Danbury, would you mind asking her to send some cold liquid refreshment out here?"

"I'll do that." Faith took her leave, winding through the gravel paths leading to the main part of the house. She couldn't resist stopping to examine a climbing fig, a coffee bush, and a vanilla orchid. *The cook can use all three of those as ingredients for tasty dishes.*

Faith decided to pop into the kitchen to pass along Sean's request. As she was pushing open the swinging door, she spotted Mrs. Danbury hustling along the corridor toward her, carrying a rattling tray. She seemed quite harried.

"Those professors really keep us busy, don't they?" Faith smiled as she held the door open for the housekeeper.

Her reward was a glare that sent prickles of embarrassment down Faith's spine.

All right, then. No joking about the employment situation.

Inside the kitchen, a stout woman with short, permed hair stood at the sink peeling potatoes. She wore a dusty pink dress, a white bib apron, thick stockings, and sensible shoes.

"Och, what do you have for me, dearie?" she asked Faith in a thick Scottish accent.

This must be Meg. Between her, Roger, and Sean, Faith felt like she was in the United Kingdom. "Sean would like a glass of something cold. He didn't say what exactly."

Mrs. Danbury sniffed. "He thinks we can read his mind." She set the tray down and unloaded the dirty dishes.

"The doctor likes iced tea, and I've got a fresh batch made just for him." Meg rinsed her hands and wiped them on a towel, then bustled toward the refrigerator.

"I'm Faith, by the way." She leaned against a counter, hoping she was out of the way. "The food so far has been delicious."

Meg smiled kindly at her. "You're the librarian from Castleton."

"I am. And it was a nice assignment to be sent here."

Mrs. Danbury snorted as she set a new tray. The kettle boiled, and she poured steaming water into a cream-colored teapot with purple flowers. It had to be a vintage Spode. Faith had seen one in an article about collectible porcelain.

Meg put the frosty glass of tea on its own little tray.

Mrs. Danbury glanced over at it, her thin lips pressed together.

"I'll take it to him," Faith said. Why not? She'd managed to supply all the professors with the books they needed, for now at least.

"That Sean. He's a right devil with the ladies." The cook set a napkin, a spoon, and a sugar dish beside the glass.

Protests rose to Faith's tongue, but she held them back. Whatever she said would sound like "the lady doth protest too much." She picked up the tray and, with a goodbye, slipped out of the kitchen.

Sean hardly noticed when she delivered the tray. *See, Meg? No flirting going on here.* She took another route back through a different part of the garden just for fun and then went to find Ava.

Her hostess was sitting in a wide wingback chair, her stockinged feet tucked under her. She looked up from her laptop with a smile. "How's it going?"

"Fine, I think," Faith said. "No one seems to need me anymore, so I was wondering if you minded if I went out for a walk."

Ava glanced toward the window, where the late-afternoon sun had finally broken through the fog. "I don't blame you for wanting to get out of the house. If I weren't at a critical spot, I'd stop and join you. Please go ahead. You're free to go anywhere, inside the house and out, but please avoid the tower."

"Thanks. I'm looking forward to exploring this beautiful property."

"We'll see you at dinner. It's at seven. And guess what? Winslow will be here." Ava's eyes glowed with happiness.

"That's great. I was hoping I'd get to meet him." Faith had left her coat upstairs, so she went up to the bedroom to dress for the outdoors. Though the sun was out, the temperature was still hovering around forty degrees, according to her phone.

As she expected, Watson was curled up on the bed. He opened one eye as she came in.

"There you are, sleepyhead. Staying out of trouble?" Faith opened the wardrobe and pulled out her coat. She also slipped on waterproof boots, mittens, and a hat.

Watson stood and stretched, his mouth open in a huge yawn.

"Want to go for a walk? It might do you good to get some fresh air." Faith also wanted Watson to learn his way around, and the best time was when she could watch him. All she needed was for him to get lost. And with his sneaky ways, keeping him inside for the full week was going to be well-nigh impossible.

To her delight, he joined her, and together owner and cat made their way down the grand staircase and out the front door. Here Faith hesitated. Which way first? To the right, where a dormant rose garden awaited? Or to the left, where an opening in a hedge beckoned?

Watson naturally chose the hedge, so Faith followed, almost trotting to keep up. Beyond the opening was a formal garden with shaped topiaries, cypress trees, and lichened statues set in niches. At one side was a long pergola wound with a huge vine, dead branches clutching the beams like clawing fingers, and in the middle sat an empty cross-shaped pool centered by a dry fountain.

Hands in pockets, Faith strolled through the garden, struck by its air of melancholy. Of course at this time of year, all gardens were somber, dull, and quiet. But even in summer, this one would be anything but cheerful. One statue was that of a tonsured monk, his finger lifted in admonition, his other arm clutching a Bible. Benches were unyielding wrought iron, as was the fountain, which featured a stone angel carrying a sword. Glancing back at the house, she saw how the garden complemented its Gothic style, completing the mood.

Watson explored the bushes while Faith continued across the garden. At the other side was another hedge, this one with an iron gate. An expanse of grass ended abruptly at a bluff. Seething ocean lay beyond, fading sunlight glimmering on the waves.

To the left, on the very edge of the cliff, stood the tower, a squat stone creation that looked transplanted from the British Isles. It had one story with arched windows and an open parapet above. Such a structure, built for decoration rather than a practical purpose, was called a folly tower.

Faith stared at the building in dark fascination, remembering the terrible stories she'd heard despite her best efforts to forget them. Violet Winterbourne was strangled, and Regina Winterbourne jumped to her death. While she stood, held in the grip of her imagination, lights flashed on in the tower.

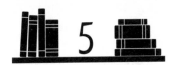

5

Lured by the lit windows, Faith crossed to the tower. *Who could be in there?* Why hadn't she seen them enter the tower? From where she stood, the hobnailed oak door was plainly visible, so it hadn't happened while she was watching.

As she drew closer, she searched for tracks in the slush but found only Watson's dainty paw prints. He was right up at the door, sniffing under the crack. Boldly Faith climbed the stone step and rapped the brass door knocker, staring up at the windows while she did so.

Nothing stirred, no face peering down—or glaring—at her impertinent interruption. Just the windows, glowing brighter as dusk descended. Then, as abruptly as they came on, the lights went out. The glass resembled blank eyes in the gray stone.

Faith shivered as a chill went down her spine. "Come on, Watson. It's time to go back to the house."

They turned toward the mansion, Faith studying the facade for an entrance. Straight ahead lay a terrace fronting the smooth expanse of lawn, a portico sheltering a series of French doors beyond. That was the room Ava had said they used for parties, adjacent to the parlor where she had been working. She'd go in that way.

They trudged through the slush, gazes fixed on their destination. The sun was setting behind a bank of gray clouds, and a brisk wind kicked up, nipping at Faith's ears and nose. Her eyes watered with cold, so she ducked her head and ran.

Watson darted past, reaching the terrace first. There he sat, in imitation of the regal lion guarding a corner.

"You are too much, Watson." She bolted into the portico and grabbed one of the door handles. She had to try three different doors, but finally one handle gave and she was inside, immersed in blessedly warm air.

Watson shot past her and disappeared into the house.

The room was dark, the only light coming from the next room through the slightly open pocket doors. Faith looked around curiously, noting the long velvet curtains edging the windows, the vast polished floor, and the small bandstand at one end. Tables and chairs were stacked along the wall, ready to be set up for a dance or a party.

As Faith walked toward the doors, she heard the low voices of a man and a woman. Ava must still be in there. When she reached for the edge of the pocket door, the words the man was speaking became clear.

"Be patient. We'll get there yet," Roger murmured.

For a split second, Faith considered staying still to hear what they were talking about, but she decided not to eavesdrop.

"Easy for you to say. You're not forced to—" Stephanie broke off as Faith opened the pocket door with a rumble. "Faith, what have you been up to?"

The assistant's disdainful glance made Faith all too conscious of how she must look, windswept with red cheeks and disheveled hair. "I was out taking a walk." To her horror, her nose began to run. Sniffling, she rooted around fruitlessly in her pockets for a tissue.

Roger presented her with a snowy white handkerchief. "You look like you could use this."

"Thanks." Faith took it gratefully and buried her face in its folds. It smelled of bay rum, an old-fashioned man's scent her father had used. "I'll give it back after it's washed."

He waved it away. "No problem. I have dozens."

"Well, I'll get out of your hair." Faith left as fast as possible without breaking into a run. She swore she could feel Stephanie's eyes boring into her back, and when she finally reached the sanctuary of the hall, she heard the woman's tinkling laughter. Faith tried to shrug off the nagging suspicion that it was aimed at her.

Winslow Winterbourne was a genial bear of a man, presiding over his dinner table as if he'd rather be nowhere else than in this room, with this group of people. Watching him bestow his undivided attention on each guest in turn, seeing how he remembered the smallest fact about everyone's lives and interests, Faith could see why Ava adored him.

Ava sat smiling at the other end of the table, her gaze rarely leaving her husband.

"So, Faith, you're the librarian at Castleton. How do you like it?" Winslow asked. He took another bite of roast beef and chewed, his eyes twinkling as he waited for her answer.

Faith squirmed a little, knowing that everyone else was listening. Against her ankles came the brush of warm fur, a sensation that relaxed her and made her smile. "I love it. My job is to care for the books and papers the library holds. I also choose books that suit the theme of each retreat and assist the attendees with using the library. I read up on every genre or author presented, of course."

Winslow stroked his short white beard. "That must be quite a range. I'm impressed."

"You must not go too deep," Roger said. "I've spent decades studying a narrow band of literature and still haven't plumbed its depths."

His comment annoyed Faith, but she didn't reply. When temperamental jostling of egos began, it was always her policy to step out of the fray.

"No doubt Faith's a quick study," Sean said, his tone pleasant.

Roger flushed at the unspoken subtext—that he wasn't—and started to protest.

But Cassandra broke in. "Now, children, don't squabble. Papa Winterbourne won't like it."

Roger subsided with a grumble.

"Cassandra's got it in her head that he looks like the older Ernest Hemingway," Sean said quietly to Faith.

Faith had to agree. Winslow did resemble the famous author.

Winslow asked Faith about some of the retreats that had been held during her tenure at Castleton. Then the discussion became general again as the group filled him in on their roles for the conference they were planning.

"They've all agreed I'm to do the keynote," Cassandra said, her smile as smug as Watson's when drinking cream.

"I'm sure you're the right choice," Winslow said. "Your work on Gothic women writers is nothing short of spectacular."

At this high praise from her publisher, Cassandra practically melted off her chair. She actually flapped a hand to cool off. "Winslow, I don't know what to say."

"Then say nothing," the acerbic Roger suggested.

Perhaps sensing the discomfort and jealousy of the others, Winslow said, "I've already got preorders for your book, Roger. Well done. And, Sean, I'd like to do the same for yours. Let me know which century it will be done so I can feature it, will you?" His boisterous laugh took the sting out of his words, and everyone joined in.

Now out of the limelight, Faith sat back and enjoyed her dinner, regarding the childish antics and one-upmanship of the others with amusement. Stephanie also had little to say. Like Ava, her attention was on Winslow, but in this case it appeared to be the vigilance of an employee toward her boss and his possible needs or requests.

By the time key lime pie came around for dessert—which sparked another thought in Faith's mind of Hemingway, who had lived in Key West—she was exhausted. Dinner had been like watching an interminable tennis match.

Excusing herself from the gathering in the library after dinner, Faith headed for her warm bed and a good book.

On the way through the hall, she ran into Mrs. Danbury, who was carrying another of her seemingly endless trays. "Mrs. Danbury, if you have a minute, I'd like to ask you something."

The woman's response was a curt nod. She stood poised to take off, like a crow perched on a branch.

"I went for a walk this afternoon and noticed there were lights on in the tower."

Mrs. Danbury's arms jerked, making the tea things rattle. "The tower, ma'am? No one is supposed to go in the tower. It's dangerous."

"Well, someone did. I saw them."

Her eyes narrowed. "You saw them?"

Faith flushed. Somehow the woman always made her feel off-balance, like she was blundering somehow. "No, not exactly. But obviously someone turned the lights on. Was it Harrison?"

An unpleasant smile slid across Mrs. Danbury's face. "Of course not. Harrison goes home after lunch. And no one goes into the tower. Ever."

An annoyed retort rose to Faith's lips, but she suppressed it with an effort. She'd ask Ava about it in the morning. "One more thing. What time is breakfast?"

"You can come down anytime you like. Meg will be happy to serve you at your convenience. The lot staying here this week likes to sleep in. So if you're an early riser, go to the kitchen."

"Thank you. I will. Good night, Mrs. Danbury."

"Good night, ma'am." As the housekeeper headed down the hall, a black-and-white blur streaked past her, fortunately not close enough to trip her, but near enough to startle her. The woman grumbled something unintelligible and went on her way.

"Watson, you naughty boy. Come on. It's time for bed."

Upstairs, Faith tidied the room and hung up discarded clothing. While checking the pockets of her jacket, her fingers encountered the sticky note she had found attached to Watson when he had accosted her ankle under the dining room table.

She glanced at it curiously. It held a string of numbers and letters, seemingly random and meaningless. Then she realized it must be someone's password. She'd give it to Ava and let her find the owner.

Faith decided to take a long soak in the big tub, making good use of the pricey lavender-scented salts provided. While in the bath, she opened the collection of short stories to one by Agatha Christie. "Philomel Cottage" was the eerie tale of a woman in danger from her husband.

Watson, curled up on the commode, kept an eye on the proceedings.

A creaking sound cut into Faith's reading. When it repeated, she sat up in the tub. Was it the wind? No. It was coming from above her head. Then she heard a couple of thuds. Footsteps.

Ava had said she heard footsteps at night, where there shouldn't be any. Had Ava been imagining them? Was Faith doing so now?

With relief, she noticed Watson was staring at the ceiling.

"You hear them too, don't you? Then I'm not crazy." *But maybe I'm jumping to conclusions. For all I know, Mrs. Danbury sleeps up there.*

When Faith finished her bath, she bundled up in a warm flannel nightgown and climbed into bed. She fluffed the pillows, pulled the covers up around her neck, snuggled into position, and lay there—wide awake.

The door behind the tapestry. Faith had forgotten all about it. She'd never be able to sleep if she could possibly be invaded at any moment. Even the thought of it made her tense up with nerves.

Gritting her teeth in annoyance, she switched on the bedside lamp and slid out of bed, carefully so as not to dislodge Watson. Barefoot on the carpet, she crossed the room and pushed aside the heavy drapery. The door was still open a crack. That was probably how Watson had gotten out earlier. *Well, at least that's one mystery solved.* Unable to resist, Faith opened it wider and peered around the edge.

In the light spilling through the doorway, Faith saw a small landing, with flights of stairs leading both downstairs and up. Maybe she could explore tomorrow, but right now she was going to lock this entrance and get into bed.

The door didn't have a lock, a bolt, or a chain. There was no way to secure it. *That's convenient.* Faith studied the furniture in her room. *The chest will work.* It held blankets and extra sheets and was heavy enough to block the door from opening all the way. At the very least, she'd be warned someone was trying to enter.

After much heaving, the chest was firmly in place, and Faith clambered back into bed and turned off the light.

Watson moved closer, nestling into the curve of her belly, and they slept.

Sunrise and Watson's insistent meowing woke her. She'd neglected to close the curtains the night before, and a panorama of sea and sky lay before her, pink and gold etching the horizon.

Watson butted her cheek with his head.

Faith gently pushed him aside. "You have food in your dish." She had put his kibble and water dishes in the bathroom, where any mess could be easily cleaned.

He thumped down from the bed, the sound disproportionate to his actual weight, and went to investigate.

Closing her eyes against the strengthening light, Faith tried to go back to sleep. But the combination of an unfamiliar place and the excitement of working with a new group of people made further rest impossible. For better or worse, she was up for the day.

The time on her phone informed her that it was probably too early to get a cup of coffee, no matter how much she would love one. Faith contented herself with reading for another half hour, then got dressed.

Faith left Watson grooming himself on the window seat and went down to the kitchen. The enticing smell of fresh-brewed coffee met her nose, but no one was in the room. Signs of breakfast preparation littered the counter—a big carton of eggs, a bowl and a whisk, a package of bacon. A radio played soft classical music.

Thinking Meg must have stepped out for a minute, Faith helped herself to coffee. She added milk from the fridge, then wandered around the kitchen, sipping her coffee. The windows looked out into a walled vegetable garden, and a back door led to a small porch and then into the enclosure.

Across from that exit was another door, which was slightly ajar. Wondering if this was the staircase that led to her room, Faith opened it.

A staircase led down to a cement-floored cellar. The light was on. A woman lay sprawled on the concrete.

Meg.

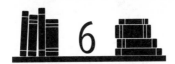

6

Faith hurried down the stairs, making sure despite her haste to grab the railing. She didn't need to slip and join the poor cook on the floor. Heart in her throat, she crouched down to examine her. Was she breathing? It was hard to tell. Faith gently pressed the artery in Meg's neck, seeking a pulse. A faint but regular beat was her reward.

Faith jumped to her feet and rushed up the steps. At the top of the stairs, she ran smack into Mrs. Danbury. "Sorry," Faith said. "We've got to call an ambulance right now. Meg fell down the stairs."

The housekeeper stared at her quizzically.

Faith pushed by her and raced for the phone. She'd noticed that the house still had a landline. She snatched the receiver and pushed the buttons, thankful there was 911 service even in a small town like Lighthouse Bay.

When the dispatcher answered, Faith gave her the information concisely. After she hung up, she told Mrs. Danbury, "They'll be here soon. Thank goodness we're not far from town."

"We'll have to open the gate," Mrs. Danbury said. She folded her arms across her chest. "It's shut and locked."

"Will you please do that and fetch your boss? I don't know which room the Winterbournes use." Faith needed to find something to put over Meg. Keeping her warm was important—she knew that much.

"Mr. Winterbourne is already gone to the airport."

Faith put her hand on the swinging door and pushed. "Okay, please tell *Mrs.* Winterbourne." What was wrong with the woman? Faith told herself not to be uncharitable. Shock affected people differently.

She dashed to the library, where she'd seen several afghans folded over the back of a sofa. She grabbed the largest one and returned to the kitchen. Mrs. Danbury was gone, and the control panel for the alarm system read *Gate Open*.

Good. Faith headed for the cellar door. As she reached it, the back door opened and Ava entered. They both recoiled in surprise.

Faith managed to speak first. "Meg's hurt, I'm taking her a blanket, and the ambulance is coming," she said, then thundered down the cellar stairs.

Ava followed. "What? Meg's hurt?" She cried out in shock when she saw her cook. "What happened?"

Faith gently placed the afghan over the woman's prone form. "I have no idea. I assume she tripped when coming down here." As she stepped back, her shoe crunched on a piece of glass. Bending closer, she spotted a broken jar of what looked like raspberry or strawberry jam sitting several feet away. *Where did that come from? Did Meg drop it or knock it over when she fell?*

A row of jam jars stood on nearby shelving along with vegetables in glass jars. Ava noticed Faith staring at the canned goods. "Meg makes jam and cans vegetables for us. Winslow loves garden-grown produce."

"There's a broken jar right there," Faith pointed out. "Be careful."

Ava hovered, fidgeting. Horror, uncertainty, and fear all flitted over her face. She glanced up the stairs. "How long until they get here?"

"I hope not long." Faith bent to check Meg's pulse again. Still steady.

A few minutes later, footsteps were heard and two EMTs carried a gurney down the stairs. Harrison accompanied them.

Faith and Ava moved aside to let the technicians do their work.

"Any idea what happened?" the taller EMT asked.

"I'm not sure," Faith said. "I looked downstairs and found her like that. I assume she fell."

The other EMT threw her a sharp glance but didn't say anything.

Harrison remained stone-faced, apparently his default expression.

"I was out on a walk. When I left, Meg was in the kitchen making breakfast. She gave me a cup of coffee just the way I like it." Ava sniffled.

"I hope she'll be all right." Tears pooled in her eyes, and she wiped them with a crumpled tissue from her pocket.

The men didn't reply as they turned their attention back to their work. Within minutes, Meg was gone, carried upstairs and loaded in the ambulance while Ava, Faith, Harrison, and Mrs. Danbury watched, Faith clutching the blanket they'd handed back to her.

"I'm going to the hospital to be with Meg," Ava said. "Can you tell the others where I am, Faith?"

"Of course," Faith said. "Please give Meg my best. I only met her yesterday, but I can tell she is a special person."

Mrs. Danbury sniffed, startling Faith. "Yes, tell her I'm worried about her. That is, if and when she wakes up." With that insensitive remark, the housekeeper stomped back toward the house, followed by Harrison, who veered off to a garden shed.

Ava stared after the housekeeper, then shook herself. "Mrs. Danbury is, um, a little different. I inherited her with the house, I'm afraid."

Faith didn't have a response for that, so she simply said, "I'll be praying for Meg. And if you hear anything new, please let us know right away."

"I will." Hunching her shoulders against the cold, Ava headed for the garage.

When Faith arrived back in the kitchen, Mrs. Danbury was beating eggs, a scowl on her face.

"You're making breakfast?" Faith asked. She'd assumed they'd all shift for themselves without the cook.

"Who else is going to do it?" the woman replied.

"Me." Faith put the blanket on a chair and moved to the toaster, which she loaded with bread slices.

"Don't put that down yet. I'll give you the signal."

Despite Mrs. Danbury's brisk manner, Faith thought the woman might actually be enjoying her company. Or that was what she chose to believe. Between the two of them, they had platters of scrambled eggs and bacon, toast, and fruit placed on the dining room table before the professors arrived.

Roger was down first, dapper in a tweed suit, freshly shaved, and hair pomaded, an effect Faith thought had died with the Victorians he studied. "This looks good," he said, picking up a serving spoon.

"I hope so," Faith said. "Mrs. Danbury cooked today."

He hesitated, the spoon dripping eggs. "Why? Did something happen to Meg?"

"Yes. She had an accident. She fell down the stairs to the basement."

His brow furrowed. "That's terrible. Was she badly injured?" He tipped the eggs onto his plate and moved on to the bacon.

"We don't know. She was unconscious."

"Who was unconscious?" Cassandra strode into the room, her heels clacking on the parquet floor. Smoothing her skirt into place, she surveyed the breakfast offerings.

"Meg," Faith said. Once again she went through the tale. As she spoke, her appetite fled, and her breakfast grew cold.

When Stephanie and Sean arrived, Faith allowed Roger and Cassandra to fill them in. They loaded their plates, grabbed coffee, and rehashed the incident numerous times while Faith sat worrying about poor Meg.

"Maybe Mrs. Danbury pushed her down the stairs," Roger said. "I heard her chewing Meg out the other day about something."

Stephanie giggled. "Maybe I should be careful. According to her, I leave too much hair in the bathtub." She patted her locks.

"Quit it, both of you," Cassandra said sharply. "It's not funny."

A moment later, Mrs. Danbury sidled in to check the platters and coffee urn.

"Are you our new cook?" Roger called out, waving a triangle of toast at her. "If so, please make the toast a little darker tomorrow." He laughed at his own poor joke.

The housekeeper bristled.

Faith said, "I made the toast. Sorry it's not to your liking." *I'll be sure to burn yours to a crisp tomorrow.* It would take more than a demanding academic to intimidate her.

"I'll fill this," Mrs. Danbury muttered, lifting the coffee urn and scurrying out.

Sensing she was upset, Faith followed, carrying her own untouched plate as an excuse.

Inside the kitchen, the housekeeper poured a fresh pot of coffee into the urn. She glanced at Faith. "Do you need something?"

"Actually, no." Faith took a breath, considering how to proceed. "I know you're really busy already and Meg being out is going to create more work."

"That's an understatement," Mrs. Danbury said. "But what can I do about it? You all need to eat." Her sour expression suggested she regarded that truth as highly unfortunate.

"I understand it will be Ava's decision, but I wanted to mention that I have a friend who is a great cook. And she might be available."

Mrs. Danbury lifted a brow.

"Her name is Brooke Milner. She's the sous-chef at Castleton Manor, which is closed this week."

The housekeeper continued to look doubtful. "You're right. It *is* up to Mrs. Winterbourne." Then her frosty demeanor thawed a bit. "But I appreciate you worrying about my workload."

And it's up to Brooke, of course. She was probably enjoying her week off. Faith sent her a text anyway, telling her she might get an offer.

Brooke texted back immediately, excited about the possibility of joining Faith. It would be fun to have Brooke at Wintersea too.

The professors spent a quiet morning working on their own projects while Faith helped them with research.

At lunchtime, an affair of sandwiches and soup Faith helped put together, Ava returned. "Hello, everyone." Patting her windblown hair into place, she took a seat at the table and selected a sandwich. "I have good news. Meg is going to be all right."

A chorus of comments and cries of relief met this news.

"Did she say what happened?" Stephanie asked.

"According to the nurse, she doesn't remember," Ava said. "I suppose that happens sometimes with a head injury. They only let me in there for two minutes to tell her we were thinking about her. And I bought her flowers and signed everyone's names."

"That was thoughtful," Cassandra said. "She certainly has always made me feel welcome here at Wintersea. And what a chef!"

Ava grimaced. "I hate to bring this up, but I don't know what we're going to do about meals. I'm not a very good cook or I'd take over."

"Maybe Cassandra can fill in," Roger said. "I heard she used to do that while in college."

Cassandra glared at him. "That's ancient history. I've hung up my apron for good."

Faith cleared her throat. "I know someone who can step in." As the others turned to stare at her in surprise, she felt her cheeks heat. "I took the liberty of asking her if she's available. Brooke Milner, the Castleton Manor sous-chef. Think of it as a preview of the conference food."

The professors looked at one another.

"I think it's a great idea," Cassandra said. "We can have her prepare samples for us so we can firm up the menu."

"All right, it's a deal," Ava said. "After lunch, can you give me her contact information, Faith? I'll see if she can come this afternoon."

"Mrs. Danbury will be happy," Sean said.

Roger scoffed. "That will be something to see."

Cassandra elbowed him. "Hush. We're lucky we have lunch."

"That's right—you are. Mrs. Danbury is very busy," Ava said. She took a bite of sandwich, chewed, and swallowed. "This afternoon, I thought we'd all keep working on our own things. I'll need Faith for a project of mine."

Roger muttered something. At Ava's sharp look, he raised his voice to ask Faith mildly, "Are you making a trip to Castleton? There are a couple of books I'd like to borrow, and Wolfe told me he wouldn't mind."

"I certainly can," Faith said. "Why don't we start a list?"

After the meal ended, Faith approached Ava. "Where are we going to be working? I'll get my computer and other things and join you."

Ava glanced around, then tugged Faith's arm, indicating they should move out of earshot. Despite the fact that the others were filing out of the room with chatter and laughter, she lowered her voice. "Meet me at my room in fifteen minutes. I'm three doors down from you, on the same side of the hallway."

Before the meeting, Faith stopped by her room for her computer and notebook. As she moved things around, she spotted the sticky note she'd meant to give to Ava. *No time like the present.* Tacking it on top of her notebook, she took it along.

A few minutes later, Faith rapped on Ava's door.

The other woman answered immediately and glanced down the hallway, nodding when she saw it was empty. "Come on in."

Why the subterfuge? Faith stepped inside, curious to see what she guessed was the master suite. Much larger than her own generous room, it was furnished in walnut and decorated in blue. The four-poster bed was curtained in velvet, and the same material adorned the tall windows overlooking the water. The carpet felt dense and springy under her shoes, like deep moss. Through an open door, Faith glimpsed another bedroom, this one decorated in burgundy. Winslow's room, she guessed, from the shoes on the carpet and other signs of use. Faith had only heard of separate bedrooms among the British nobility or the very rich.

"You can leave your things here," Ava said, making room on the round table by the windows. Her computer was already set up, and a stack of books stood next to it.

Faith set her items down, pulled off the note, and handed it to Ava. "I think someone dropped this. It might be important, so I'm giving it to you."

Ava glanced at the note, started to put it aside, then brought it back for a closer look. She waved it at Faith. "Where did you get this?" Her voice held an odd note of tension.

"It was stuck on Watson's fur yesterday at lunch. I don't know where *he* got it."

The other woman's gaze darted around as though she didn't know what to do first. "You're coming with me."

"Where are we going?"

"Regina's room." Her eyes lit up with something close to defiance.

As they went down the hall to another wing, Ava told Faith that the rooms she and Winslow now used had belonged to Winslow's sisters. "This family had the tradition of separate bedrooms for men and women. Regina's room belonged to Winslow's mother and grandmother."

"Why aren't you using it then?" Faith blurted out.

Ava shook her head, frowning. "Mrs. Danbury keeps it exactly as Regina had it. When we got married, I suggested moving in, but her reaction—and Winslow's—made me drop the topic."

Regina's room was in one of the turrets, Faith realized once Ava opened the door. The room was round, lined with windows on three sides. The room had the ambience of an enchanted bower with its pink silk drapes and bedding, shell-white furniture, and fireplace. The furniture was delicate and finely carved.

It was also a shrine to Winslow's late wife. Pictures of Regina and Winslow stood on the mantel and on the bedside table. A silver brush set and perfume bottles were laid out on a pretty vanity, complete with a bench covered in a tufted cushion.

Ava crossed to a door and opened it. "Look. All her clothes are still here."

The dressing room was lined with racks, rows of shoes placed underneath. At the far end was a set of drawers. Through another door was a bathroom, tiled in pale pink. Toiletries and soaps lined the shelves and bathtub.

Faith was bewildered. "I don't understand this. I mean, I can understand it for a while after she died but now?"

"I know. It's strange." Ava's bottom lip trembled. "I don't know what to do. Winslow gets so upset when I mention her name. I've given up."

"I can understand your reluctance to press the topic. Under the circumstances, it's a tough subject." Suicide was often difficult for family members to cope with, often such a loaded subject that they avoided the mere mention of the deceased.

"Sometimes I wonder . . ." Ava strolled over to Regina's desk, where she opened a drawer and rummaged through the contents. She cast Faith a glance. "What if she didn't kill herself?"

Faith's heart lurched. "What do you mean?"

"What if someone killed her?" Ava closed the first drawer, then moved to the next. "I don't believe she committed suicide."

Faith struggled to find words. "But surely they would be able to tell if it was murder."

Ava shrugged one shoulder, intent on sorting through several flash drives she had discovered. "Maybe. She fell off the tower onto the rocks. Who's to say she wasn't pushed?" She picked up a blue flash drive and held it out so Faith could see it. "You know that sticky note you found? I think it could be the password to Regina's book."

7

Faith joined Ava at the desk. She pointed to the sticky note now resting beside the flash drive. "You really think it's the password to that drive?"

Ava nodded. "Regina was working on a book, one that Winslow was going to publish. I bet Watson found the note in one of the books she would have used for reference. I should have thought to look there myself."

"What about the other flash drives?" Faith asked.

Ava gathered the other drives, then shoved them back into a drawer. "None of these have anything important on them. I checked them ages ago. But this blue one is locked." She pointed to the letters and numbers on the note that read *27CL5BRW*. "Before she married Winslow, Regina lived at 27 Clancy Street, apartment 5B. RW? That's self-explanatory."

Faith's spine prickled. "Should we open her private files?" Part of her was appalled at the idea of prying into a dead woman's thoughts, but on the other hand, what if Ava was right? There might be clues to Regina's death in the manuscript.

"I feel kind of squishy about it, but I think we need to. What if someone was threatening her or something?" Ava shivered. "What if *she* heard footsteps and had strange things happen to her?"

"Good point." Faith looked around. "There isn't a computer in here."

"Winslow has it. And, no, the book isn't on there. I checked." Ava picked up the password and flash drive. "Let's go try mine."

On the way back to Ava's room, a sense of secretive, exhilarated haste fueled Faith's movements. She often had a similar feeling when she was on the trail of obscure and exciting information while doing research. She imagined she was like a cat tracking prey, tantalizing scents leading her on.

Ava inserted the flash drive into her laptop, and when the screen came up, she entered the password. "Keep your fingers crossed. I might be totally wrong—no, wait. Here it is." She turned the computer so Faith could see it too.

A document was displayed on the screen. Ava checked the properties. "This was last updated on August 15, two and a half years ago."

"How close is . . . ?" Faith's voice trailed off. She couldn't bring herself to finish the question.

"The day before Regina died." Ava scanned the beginning sentences. Her brows rose. "Listen to this. 'Violet Winterbourne was brutally murdered on a hot summer night at her shorefront estate. As the sun sank in a glory of red and gold, an unknown assailant accosted the socialite in the stone tower overlooking the cliffs. This was Violet's favorite place, the retreat where she listened to classical music, read books, and enjoyed her priceless porcelain collection.' It goes on like that."

"She was writing about Winslow's grandmother."

"It looks that way." Ava scrolled down. "Ooh, listen to this. 'Some houses are more than buildings, far greater than the sum of bricks and shingles and wood that create a haven from the elements. Wintersea is one such place. With its turrets and pointed windows, its stone folly and formal gardens, the mansion is a reflection of the man who built it, the eccentric Cedric Winterbourne, inventor and poet. After making his fortune in railroads, Cedric retired to this slice of coastline and built a house that reflected both his dreams and nightmares, according to his diary.'"

"That's fascinating." Faith knew that people built houses from various motivations, to shelter a family or to express their taste and wealth. But she'd never heard the design process expressed quite like this.

Ava sucked in a breath. "You won't believe this. 'I myself have fallen under the spell of Wintersea. I wander its hallways, climb the tower, gaze at the ever-changing ocean and the sky in amazement and gratitude. But I also sense the dark side, the stuff of Cedric's nightmares. Something is very wrong at Wintersea, and Violet was merely its first victim.'"

Faith gulped. "I wonder what Regina was talking about."

"So do I." Ava blinked away tears. "Perhaps weird things happened to her too."

"She never mentioned anything?"

"I didn't see her very often, and we weren't that close anymore." Lost in thought, Ava stared at the screen. "Unless she talks about it here, we may never know. Let me read the last entry." She rolled the cursor to the bottom.

She read, "'Today was gorgeous, absolutely perfect. Winslow and I went for a sail in *Lightning*, then came back to get ready for our weekend guests, who are arriving tomorrow morning. Meg procured fresh haddock, and we had that for dinner on the terrace.' There's nothing that sounds like she was thinking about death."

"You're right. There isn't. But maybe some of the other chapters have clues."

Ava moved the cursor up and down the list of entries. "It will take ages to read all this." Her shoulders slumped in discouragement.

"I'll do it," Faith said. "I know you're busy with your dissertation."

"Would you? I'd appreciate that." Ava copied the file to her computer, then handed Faith the drive. "Let me know what you learn." Her phone dinged, and she pulled it out of her pocket. "Good news. Your friend has agreed to cook for us. She'll be here in fifteen minutes." Then the phone rang, right in Ava's hand. "Sorry, Faith," she said. "I have to take this."

Without ever learning what project Ava had wanted Faith's assistance with in the first place, Faith returned to her room and took out her laptop. She made a copy on the hard drive and e-mailed herself another for a backup. After a disaster or two, she'd learned her lesson and always made backups.

Glancing at the time, she gave a yelp. Brooke would be arriving any minute. Thinking fast, she hid the drive under the mattress, planning to give it back to Ava later.

As Faith lurked in the hall, waiting for Brooke by the front door, she studied the art on the walls and the contents of a locked cabinet filled with porcelain figurines. *The remains of Violet's collection?* Faith didn't collect figurines, but she had to admire the delicacy and artfulness of the workmanship. They were most likely rare and valuable.

The doorbell bonged, a sonorous note that echoed.

Faith rushed to answer the door, revealing Brooke on the steps, suitcase and tote in hand and a huge smile on her face.

Brooke entered, peering around curiously. "I've always wanted to see inside this house. From the outside, it has such atmosphere." She dropped her bags on the floor.

Mrs. Danbury appeared, moving with her eerie gliding gait. "I see you got here before I did," she said to Faith, her tone disapproving.

Brooke's expression when she took in the housekeeper's formal garb and stern demeanor was almost comical.

Faith hid a smile. "Mrs. Danbury, this is Brooke Milner, our temporary cook. Brooke, Mrs. Danbury takes excellent care of us here."

"Nice to meet you." Brooke thrust out her hand, only to have Mrs. Danbury regard it dubiously. Brooke withdrew the hand. "Well, yes. I'm glad to be here. Perhaps you can show me the way to the kitchen."

Mrs. Danbury glanced down at Brooke's belongings, and, as if by osmosis, Harrison entered the hallway.

Brooke stared at him in fascination as he bent to gather her bags.

"She's in the lavender room, Harrison," Mrs. Danbury said. "Now if you'll follow me, Miss Milner."

Brooke gave Faith a shrug. "I'll see you later."

"Let's get together after dinner." Faith smiled. "I'm looking forward to seeing what you come up with." She knew her friend would impress the professors with her cooking prowess, a foretaste of the conference to come.

After Mrs. Danbury and Brooke disappeared into the house, Ava came down the stairs. "Can you please go to Castleton Manor for me?" She handed Faith a list. "We need these books."

"Sure. I can do that right now." Faith tucked the list into her pocket, then went upstairs to fetch her purse. Watson was napping on the window seat, and she paused to pat him. "I'm going to Castleton for a little while, but I'll be back before supper. Be a good boy, okay?"

Watson opened one eye as if to say, "When am I not?" He displayed his pink tongue in a yawn, then snuggled down again, head on his paws.

Faith found herself yawning in response. "Oh, that's catching." She eyed her comfy bed. "I better get out of here before I'm tempted to join you." The stresses and strains of the day had worn her out. She picked up her purse. Maybe if she hurried, she would have time to nap before dinner. "Bye, Watson," she called, closing the door softly.

The doorknob rattled and the cat lifted his head, expecting to see his human. She'd probably forgotten something, which happened often, or perhaps she needed another glimpse of his face, which other humans called "cute." He didn't blame her if that was the case. She had been far too busy, and frankly, he was feeling neglected.

His fur stood on end. It was that tall human with the severe face who didn't seem to like anyone, including him. The cat slid off the bed and landed silently on the carpet, something he'd been practicing in secret.

From under the bed, he watched as the human carried in a pile of fluffy towels. He liked sleeping on towels, especially when they were warm from the dryer.

A few seconds later, she emerged from the tiled lair, her feet clumping across the rug in thick-soled shoes. He didn't like those shoes. They were the kind that stepped on cat's paws.

What was she doing? He crept out, remaining in the shadow of the nightstand as the tall human went to the tapestry covering the secret entrance. She pulled it aside with a grunt and frowned at the chest blocking the door. Then she dropped the tapestry with a huff, whirling around to study the rest of the room.

The cat edged into the shadows, the human's rapier gaze barely grazing him. She went over to the table, where his human's computer sat open, the screen blank. "Asleep," she called it, as he wanted to be. If only the rude interruption would end. The human gave a disgusted sniff at the state of the computer.

When she turned and stepped toward the bed, he held his breath. Had she seen him? Irritated at his failure, he tensed, ready to run.

But to his relief, she bent and thrust her hands under the mattress. She pulled out the object his human had hidden. She examined it and moved it toward her pocket. Then, thinking better of it, she replaced it under the mattress just so.

The cat gave the tall human points for that. He hadn't quite perfected that trick while snooping.

Even though she'd been away only one night, Faith found herself seeing Castleton Manor afresh. *What a fantastic place it is,* she thought as she pulled into the employee parking lot, *huge and gorgeous—but also home.* That realization startled her, and she laughed. Wintersea was beautiful too but slightly strange. There were tense undercurrents that worked on the nerves. In contrast, Castleton was dignified and gracious, its atmosphere promising rest and peace.

Most of the time.

Marlene Russell popped out from nowhere and advanced on Faith's SUV, waving both arms in wide arcs.

Faith opened the door and stepped out. "What's going on?"

"I thought you were away for the week." Marlene put her hands on her hips and glared, as if Faith were breaking some rule of protocol.

"I am. I just came back for some library books. Wolfe said Ava could borrow them," she added hastily, not wanting Marlene to think she was acting without proper authority. "So what's up?" she asked again. Surely Marlene hadn't accosted her to ask such an unimportant question.

"We've got a crisis. You know the man who came to tune up the boiler? Well, he broke it."

"Oh no. That's terrible." Castleton's boiler provided heat as well as vast quantities of hot water for showers, laundry, cooking, and cleaning.

"Water leaked into the library from one of the radiators. It was spitting everywhere." Marlene's eyes gleamed with the relish of one who enjoyed relaying bad news.

"What? Are any books damaged?" Faith tensed, ready to bolt toward the precious collection.

Marlene chuckled. "Everything is fine. Not a single page got wet. But the carpet was soaked, and we're having it lifted and cleaned. You might have bare floorboards in there for a while."

Faith's heart slowed to a reasonable rate. "We can live with that."

"Good." Marlene's nod was decisive. "You might have to." She flapped one hand. "I'm off. See you." She marched toward her car, parked across the lot.

Faith went in the opposite direction, toward the front of the manor. The day was cold, with a nasty little breeze that crept up pant legs and down coat collars. Inside was no better, the lack of heat already evident in a chill that penetrated Faith's bones. Keeping her coat on, she strode through the empty rooms.

The door to the library was open, a rare occurrence because it was kept locked to protect valuable books and manuscripts from improper handling or theft. Maybe the workmen were still in there dealing with the carpet.

But the library was empty and dark, except for the lone male figure seated in one of the armchairs. A single bulb lit his salt-and-pepper hair. Wolfe Jaxon.

Faith hesitated in the doorway, not wanting to bother her boss.

Wolfe must have sensed her presence because he turned his head and saw her, his blue eyes piercing despite the gloom. "Come on in." He gestured at the floorboards, the area where the rug had been clearly visible due to a difference in the color of the wood. "You can see we had a little accident."

"Marlene told me. I'm glad the books weren't affected." Faith started to unbutton her coat but then thought better of it. It was freezing in here without the boiler operating.

Wolfe glanced down at a piece of paper in his lap.

Faith asked, "What's that? An estimate of the bill?"

"Nothing so wonderfully mundane, I'm afraid." He picked up the sheet by one corner. "I'm being blackmailed."

8

Faith wasn't sure she'd heard him correctly. "Did you say—?"

Wolfe's laugh was hollow. "That I'm being blackmailed? Yes. Come take a look."

Her pulse racing with trepidation, Faith quickly crossed the floor to his side and read the note.

You were there when she died. Pay up or else I will go to the media. Don't even think about going to the police.

Faith's knees wobbled. "What is this? Who died? Why do they want *you* to pay?"

"Have a seat and I'll tell you." Wolfe motioned to a nearby armchair.

She perched on the edge, hands gripped in her lap, finding herself leaning forward with shoulders hunched in anxiety.

In contrast, Wolfe slumped back in the chair, his handsome face etched with lines Faith had never noticed. "You know I was once engaged?"

Faith nodded. One of the first stories she'd heard at Castleton Manor was how Wolfe's fiancée, a model named Valentina Pestova, had died five years before in a boating accident. Ever since, the multimillionaire, widely considered one of the state's most eligible bachelors, had dated but kept his heart guarded, giving rise to speculation about whether he would ever fully move on from his tragic loss.

"Everyone talked about how beautiful Valentina was. But that wasn't why I—she was sweet and caring and . . . nice. She was truly and deeply a good person."

Faith, who had only seen photos of the spectacular model, was touched. It appeared Wolfe had loved Valentina for herself, not just her looks.

"But she wasn't perfect. She had a temper." He laughed ruefully. "And we argued."

No, not the perfect couple! Faith was further reassured by this confession of normality by what must have been the East Coast's most famous fairy-tale pairing. She shifted in her seat, not sure why he was telling her all this.

"There's a point. I promise." Wolfe paused. "I let Valentina and her friends borrow my yacht for a couple of days. They were cruising around the Maine islands, celebrating a birthday. All the women were to be in the wedding party, you see, and they were also planning the event."

"And that's where she—?"

"Yes. That night Valentina fell off the boat, hitting her head in the process. The captain didn't even notice, so he was fired of course." He pressed his lips together. "And I always felt responsible. It happened on my watch, so to speak. I should never—" He broke off.

Faith's thoughts went back to the note. "Whoever wrote that thinks you were there. But you weren't, right? You would have rescued her."

Wolfe bent his head, making a sound oddly like a muffled sob. "Of course I would have." He put a hand over his eyes and rubbed. "I wasn't officially on the cruise, but I did intercept the boat in the early evening when they were anchored off an island harbor. The exact time she fell was never officially determined, so the blackmailer is putting two and two together and getting an accusation of murder."

"But surely the others noticed that she was alive when you left." At the expression on his face, Faith's pulse ratcheted up a notch. "Tell me they did." She realized her voice was becoming shrill and forced herself to take a deep breath.

"No. We argued about something trivial, and I took off. The other women said they didn't hear my boat leave, so it was a while before they went looking for her. About an hour, I figure. They were playing music in the saloon."

"What about the crew?"

"They were in their quarters, playing cards. Didn't hear a thing. They claimed they didn't even hear me arrive. Or leave. To be fair, there were other boats buzzing around the bay. It's popular."

Faith pictured the scene in her head. The women laughing and chattering belowdecks, trying not to intrude upon Valentina and Wolfe. The argument. He stormed away and then what? She slipped and fell overboard? How? They might never know.

A nasty little suspicion whispered in her mind. She repelled it immediately. *No way. Wolfe is innocent.* He was far too decent a man to kill someone.

A rock formed in her belly as she asked, "The police never questioned your movements or involvement?" Questioning her boss about such matters was awkward. To make it worse, he didn't answer right away. She hastily added, "If they cleared you, what can the blackmailer do?"

"The short answer is a lot of damage, especially to Castleton and my other companies." Wolfe paused. "I did my best to keep this out of the tabloids and succeeded. And, yes, I was cleared, as you put it." His eyes flashed, and Faith quailed a little. "I gave them the timing of my movements, and they accepted it. The medical examiner said Valentina's injury was consistent with a fall. She hit her temple just right."

Faith winced. "I'm so sorry," she murmured. "I know this is painful."

"It's not your fault. It's the fault of whoever did this." Wolfe flicked the paper with his finger. "Seeing it opens up all the old wounds." He gave her a crooked smile. "Wounds I thought had healed."

Their eyes met for a long moment. Faith felt her face heat . . . with what? Surely Wolfe wasn't interested in her, a plain librarian, after his sweet, glamorous model. Not that she wanted him to be. She tore her gaze away, feigning great interest in her laced hands. "It must be someone who was there," she said.

"That's what I think." Wolfe's tone was grim. "I'm going to figure out who and put a stop to this nonsense." His somber expression relaxed into a smile. "You're good at solving mysteries. Maybe you can help me."

Wolfe excused himself to take a business call, and Faith got to work on the task that had brought her to the manor. All the while she was pulling books from the shelves for Ava, she pondered Wolfe's situation.

How strange for someone to come out of the woodwork now. Maybe the blackmailer thought of the high-profile Wolfe as easy pickings.

A short while later, Faith packed the stack of books in a tote and locked the library, then hurried to her vehicle. She felt bad about leaving without saying goodbye to Wolfe, but she didn't want to interrupt whatever work he was probably doing now. Besides, she was chilled to the bone and eager to get back to Wintersea.

By the time she drove through the gate, an early dusk was falling, marked by bruise-colored clouds creeping in from the west, a sign of bad weather to come. The woods surrounding the house were sunk in gloom, but as she turned the last corner, a shaft of light pierced the overcast skies and touched the house with gold. The chimneys poured smoke, a promise of the warmth inside. Faith thought of Brooke in the kitchen and wondered how she was faring in her new position.

As she pulled up in front of the house, Faith spotted Ava and Sean emerging through the break in the hedge.

Heads close together, they were conversing intimately and seemed not to notice her arrival. Partway across the lawn, they stopped walking and turned to each other, their faces white ovals in the fading light. Ava spoke passionately, waving one arm for emphasis, while Sean stared down at her. Then, to Faith's shock, he took her in his arms, burying his face in her hair.

Faith couldn't look away in spite of the disagreeable sensation that she was behaving like a Peeping Tom.

Ava struggled in Sean's arms, and after a moment, he released her. With a toss of her head, she spun around and stalked away, heading for the front of the house—and Faith.

Faith hastily turned her head and pretended to be busy retrieving her items from the passenger seat. Then she opened the driver's door and slid out, bringing her tote and purse.

"Faith, you made it." Ava smiled as she crossed the remaining strip of lawn to the driveway. "How was Castleton?"

"Freezing. The boiler went out." Faith gladly played along, eager to act as if she hadn't witnessed the encounter. She noticed that Sean had slipped back through the hedge.

"Oh, that's terrible. Will it be fixed soon?" Ava fell into step beside Faith as she went up the front path.

"I'm sure it will. Wolfe is aware of the problem, and you know how efficient he is." As Faith chattered, the memory of what she'd just seen played in her mind. Ava had rejected Sean vehemently. *Or had she?* Maybe Faith's arrival wasn't as unobtrusive as she'd believed. With difficulty, she pushed away these unpleasant thoughts. Whatever was going on was none of her business.

Gusts of toasty air hit their faces when they entered the house. Maybe Faith could warm up at last. Faith and Ava took off their coats and hung them in the closet.

"Does Harrison work part-time?" Faith asked. She'd wondered if the man would greet them at the door, as he did sometimes.

"He does in the winter and spring." Ava kicked off her shoes and slid into slippers. "He's in charge of the gardens, so he works full days in the summer."

"Has he been here a long time?" Faith picked up her purse and the tote of books.

Ava turned her head quickly. "Yes, he has. Are you thinking—?"

Cassandra sauntered into the foyer and stopped, planting her hands on her hips. "There you are, Faith. I've been waiting all afternoon for you to get back. I'm totally stuck without one of those books." She smiled, but Faith had the impression that she was irritated.

Faith felt as if she'd been scolded. She counted to ten, annoyed at the woman's attitude. She'd done the professors a favor by traipsing to Castleton Manor, as had Wolfe by letting them take books off the premises. "Then I'm glad the Castleton library had it and I had time to get it for you. Give me a minute and I'll meet you in the library."

"I'll join you two shortly," Ava said. She patted the pockets of her pants with a frown, then opened the closet door again and searched her coat pockets.

"What's the matter?" Cassandra's upper lip curled. "Did you lose something?"

Ava's motions were frantic now as she patted her pants once more. "My phone. I can't find it." She swiveled toward the front door. "I hope I didn't drop it outside."

"Let's call it," Faith said. She set down the tote and rummaged for her own phone in her purse. "I lose my phone all the time."

Cassandra shrugged and turned to go. "I'll meet you in the library."

Faith dialed Ava's number and put the phone to her ear. "It's ringing."

Ava shook her head. "I don't hear it anywhere, and we would if it was down here. My ringtone is Beethoven's Fifth." She grabbed her coat. "I'd better go out and look for it."

"Do you want my help?" Faith didn't want to go out in that dank cold air again, but she felt obliged to offer.

"No, please don't bother. Go get warm by the fire."

In the library, Faith carried the tote to a table and began unloading the books.

The room was empty except for Cassandra, who was leaning on the mantel and staring into the leaping flames. "Did Ava find her phone?"

"Not yet." Faith pulled the last volume out of the bag. "Which book did you want?"

Cassandra joined her, pouncing on a scholarly work about the female Gothic in the domestic sphere that was written in the early 1900s. She picked up the book, cradling it in the crook of her arm. She turned to go, then paused, studying Faith with narrowed eyes, a small smile playing on her lips.

"Can I help you with something else?" Faith asked. She gestured at the other tomes. "Do you need another book?"

Cassandra shook her head, making her dangling earrings jingle.

She inhaled deeply, then said, "I've been debating whether to say something, but after that scene in the hall, I must." She stepped closer, lowering her voice. "Ava is . . . well, let's just say she's always having a problem with something or other."

Affronted because she liked her hostess and sympathized with her difficult position as second wife, Faith said, "What on earth do you mean?"

Cassandra pursed her lips. "I don't mean anything, really." Her tone implied that Faith had taken offense needlessly. "It's simply that Ava's a bit of a drama queen. Everything is a crisis. And most of the time, it's all up here." She tapped her temple. "So take it with a grain of salt." She spun around, her skirts swirling, and strode elegantly from the room.

Why did Cassandra feel compelled to tell me that? How rude, considering Ava is hosting her so generously. Thrusting aside the puzzle of discourteous, ungrateful guests, Faith gravitated to the roaring fire. Her duty done, she was going to focus on warming up for a while.

"What is this?" Roger asked, inhaling the steam from the savory chicken dish Brooke placed in front of him. He rolled his eyes in ecstasy. "It smells heavenly."

Brooke maintained her professional demeanor, but her sparkling eyes revealed she was thrilled. The sous-chef adored it when people enjoyed her creations. "A simple, classic recipe. Chicken marsala. If you like it, I'll suggest to the executive chef that we have it at the conference." She continued around the table, placing a plate in front of each person.

Faith stared at her serving hungrily, awaiting the signal from their hostess to begin. Tender egg noodles and steamed broccoli crowns nestled next to the chicken, which was drenched in a rich sauce with plenty of fresh mushrooms.

"Thank you, Brooke. This looks delightful," Ava said. Despite her complimentary words, she merely toyed with her fork, staring into space. "Dig in, everyone."

With noises of appreciation and pleasure, the diners obeyed.

Sean offered the bread basket to Faith. "Roll?"

"Thanks." Not meeting his eyes, she selected one—soft and warm to the touch—and broke it open, then applied a pat of butter, which began to melt immediately. She'd flinched when Sean had chosen the seat next to her, remembering the inappropriate scene in the garden. Now she was hyperaware of his every movement.

After passing the basket on, Sean brought a forkful of chicken and mushrooms to his lips, chewed, and swallowed. "Scrumptious."

As for Ava, she remained distracted, picking at her food. She avoided Faith's end of the table, focused instead on Roger as he rambled on in excruciating detail about a talk he had given at a London literary club.

Faith was using the last morsel of chicken to mop up as much of the leftover sauce on her plate as she could when a series of heavy notes rang out.

Ava dropped her fork. "That's my phone. Where is it?" She leaped up from her chair and dashed around the room, searching as the notes continued to sound. "Ah, there it is." She snatched it up from a ceramic bowl on the sideboard. Instantly it was quieter. The bowl had amplified the sound of the ringtone. "How did it get here?"

"You must have left it during lunch," Stephanie said.

Ava knit her brows. "But I remember using it after that." She studied the screen as if the phone could somehow tell her what had happened.

"Who called?" Roger asked. He nudged Cassandra with his elbow. "Godot?" He laughed at his own poor joke, which referenced the Samuel Beckett play *Waiting for Godot*.

Ava carried the phone back to the table. "No one. Not anyone I recognize, anyway." She shook her head as if trying to clear her confusion.

"Probably a telemarketer," Cassandra said. "I hate it when they get your cell number."

Brooke entered the dining room and started clearing plates. "We've got warm pecan pie and vanilla bean ice cream for dessert. Who would like some?"

Groans and protests met her offer, but almost everyone said yes, including Faith. Brooke's desserts were to die for, and Faith couldn't resist despite her tight waistband.

Thinking Brooke could use a hand, Faith excused herself and went to the kitchen. "How's it going?" she asked her friend.

Brooke looked up from the pie she was slicing. "Great. Did you like the meal?"

"I loved it. And I think everyone else did too."

"Judging by the empty plates, it seems so." She nodded at the coffee brewing on a two-pot machine. "Will you fill those carafes? I made decaf and regular. I'm not using the urn because people aren't going to drink much this late."

"I'd be happy to." Faith poured steaming coffee into two carafes, grateful for the different-colored handles that would denote decaf and regular.

Brooke dropped her voice to a conspiratorial tone. "Want to get together after dinner and do a little exploring?" She winked. "Castleton Manor isn't the only house with secrets."

9

Faith stared at her friend in astonishment. "You've been here only a few hours. How did you have time to find out anything at all?"

"I'm good," Brooke said smugly. Then she relented. "Actually, I picked Mrs. Danbury's brain. She told me this place is riddled with secret staircases and tunnels. She invited me to check them out."

Brooke getting Mrs. Danbury to talk was incredible, but Faith's mind fastened on one mystery solved. "The tower," she said. The lack of footprints at the front entrance made sense if someone went in a different way.

"I have no idea what you're talking about, but you owe me a long debriefing session. I don't even know what happened to Meg." Brooke made a shooing motion at Faith. "Take the coffee out. I'll be right behind you with the dessert."

Faith ate her pecan pie in record time, barely tasting its melt-in-your-mouth sweetness. Despite earlier protests, everyone around the table cleaned their plates. Roger and Sean even went back for seconds. Brooke gladly gave them another piece, agreeing the pie needed to be on the conference menu.

"As the planning committee, we should get a whole pie to ourselves," Roger said in an attempt to negotiate. "That will be two pieces each."

"That's up to the bosses," Brooke said with a wink. "Ava and Cassandra." Objections followed from the men while Ava and Cassandra preened.

"We'll let you have pie if you're good," Ava said.

"Oh, I'm good, baby," Roger said, attempting to sound roguish.

The women jeered and hooted in response, to everyone's laughter.

"I like the new chef," Cassandra said after Brooke went back to the kitchen. "She makes a job that can sometimes be difficult seem like fun."

That's right. Cassandra used to work as a cook when she was in college. "I think Brooke genuinely enjoys both cooking and interacting with people," Faith said. "It's a winning combo."

Roger patted his belly. "It's working for me. Bring it on."

The scholars adjourned to the library with coffee, and Faith helped Brooke clean up. They loaded the dishwasher and put away the few leftovers. Faith wiped her hands on a towel and removed the apron Brooke had insisted she wear to protect her clothing. "All right, I'm ready to see the hidden passages."

Brooke put up a hand. "Not so fast." She refilled their mugs with decaf coffee and pulled out a chair at the kitchen table. "I want to hear everything."

Faith took a seat. Cocking her head, she smiled at her friend. "Shall I start with the mysterious footsteps overhead, the fact that Winslow's first wife's room is a shrine, or that something . . . irregular seems to be happening between Ava and Sean? Not to mention Meg's accident and the lights in the tower."

Oh, and Wolfe is being blackmailed. With an effort, Faith held back the words. That wasn't related to what was going on here at Wintersea, and Wolfe had told her about his situation in confidence.

Now Brooke was the one who was amazed. "All that happened since yesterday? Good thing you called me in for reinforcements." She got up and rummaged through the cupboards. "And I have a feeling this discussion will require a second dessert." She opened a tin. "Molasses cookies made by Meg, I assume." She grabbed one and took a big bite. "They're delicious."

The chewy, spicy cookies were indeed delectable, and Faith ate a couple of them as she took Brooke through the events at Wintersea in chronological order, deciding that was the best approach rather than jumping around by subject matter. Finally Faith ground to a halt, her throat dry with talking so much.

Brooke gave the verdict: "There's something strange going on here."

Faith burst out laughing. "No kidding. But I have no idea how it all ties together. And poor Ava is going crazy."

"I can't imagine marrying a man who keeps his first wife's bedroom intact." Brooke shivered. "How creepy is that?"

"Very." Faith slid the tin of cookies out of reach. "Let's get going. If I can manage to waddle up and down the stairs." She suppressed a slight feeling of discomfort at creeping around Ava's house. But Mrs. Danbury had encouraged them to explore. Well, she had encouraged Brooke, anyway.

Brooke pushed her chair back. "The exercise will do you good." She carried their mugs to the sink and put the cookies away, then foraged in a drawer for a flashlight. She waved it at Faith. "Come into my lair," she intoned in a deep voice.

Laughing, Faith followed her to a door in one corner of the kitchen. "What's this, the broom closet?" she joked.

"Be patient, my pretty." Brooke turned the knob. "Mrs. Danbury said this was the servants' staircase."

Through the door was a landing, with flights leading up and down.

Faith pointed up. "This must be the staircase Mrs. Danbury uses to get to my room."

"Let's find out." Turning on the flashlight, Brooke led the way.

The steps were short and the enclosure narrow, an effect that made Faith feel rather claustrophobic. The walls and ceiling were painted light tan, which resulted in the space feeling depressing to boot.

At the top of the steps, a passage with a low ceiling led to the right. Brooke shone the light down the hallway, revealing a line of doors. At the end was another staircase rising into the darkness.

"I wonder which one is mine," Faith said. "The others must go to bedrooms too."

Brooke stepped close to the first door and pressed her ear against the wood.

"What are you doing?"

"Listening." Brooke made a come-on gesture.

With a slight feeling of trepidation, Faith leaned her head against the door. Faint meowing met her ears. "Watson." She turned the knob and pushed, only to be met with resistance provided by the chest she'd shoved against it.

The door moved only a couple of inches, but that barrier was no match for the cat. He thrust his head through and then the rest of his body.

"Looks like we have a companion on our travels," Brooke said. She squatted down and stroked Watson's back.

He purred, rubbing his full length against her legs.

"As long as he doesn't get lost in here," Faith said.

Watson glanced up at her, then trotted down the hall.

"If this place is anything like Castleton," Brooke said, "I'm sure he already knows his way around better than anyone else."

"You're probably right." As they reached the second door, Faith said, "I have no idea who has this bedroom. I do know Ava and Winslow are at the end."

Once again Brooke pressed her ear to the door. "Three guesses."

This time Faith heard singing, a clear tenor belting out an Irish ballad. She jerked back, feeling intrusive. "Sean's room must be next to mine."

Brooke looked her up and down. "Lucky you. You can arrange all kinds of accidental meetings in the corridors."

Faith shook her head. Brooke was always trying to jump-start Faith's romantic life. Usually it was their boss Wolfe in her sights. Now it was the handsome professor.

"He's gorgeous. And that accent." Gazing upward, Brooke patted her chest. "I could listen to it all day."

"He's interested in Ava, remember?" Faith scanned the dark corridor for Watson. Where was he?

Brooke made a scoffing sound. "That's going nowhere. She's married. You can swoop right in and make him forget all about her."

"Oh, give it up. Let's go find Watson."

They located him at the end of the hall, perched on the bottom step of the staircase leading up. When they reached him, he turned and began to climb. These stairs weren't any wider—if anything, they were a little narrower.

"The servants certainly didn't live in the lap of luxury," Brooke said when they achieved the top.

She was right. On both sides of the hallway were tiny rooms, some still furnished with metal bed frames and warped bureaus, the drawers hanging open. A porcelain chamber pot and basin with pitcher in one room illustrated how long ago they had been used.

"I'll bet the footsteps I heard were made by someone nosing around up here. But I can't imagine what they would be looking for." Faith entered one of the rooms, noting the peeling floral wallpaper someone had put up in an attempt to brighten the place.

"I hear you." Brooke shuddered. "These rooms are hideous. And they're not even warm, which you'd think they would be, being on the third floor."

In one window, a dingy rag of a curtain blew slightly, confirming Brooke's words. Faith assumed that cold air leaked around the old panes.

"Let's go," Faith said, anxious to go back downstairs to warmth and light. "Where's Watson?"

Brooke pointed with her flashlight. He was sitting on one of the few mattresses left, grooming himself. "Come on, Watson. We've got miles to go before it's time to wash up."

Faith was startled. "What do you mean?"

"We came up, and now we're going down."

Bemused, Faith followed Brooke back to the main level, then farther down to the basement.

Watson trailed them, stopping now and then to sniff at something.

A door at the bottom of the steps opened into the basement, next to the shelves of canned goods. The overhead lights weren't switched on, so Brooke's flashlight was necessary and welcome. She aimed it around the room, touching on the boiler and the shelves filled with canned goods and other household items.

As glass glinted in the pale light, an idea struck Faith. "Meg was on her way up, not down."

"What are you talking about?" Brooke trained the light on Faith, careful not to hit her in the eyes, which she appreciated.

Faith pointed to the line of glass jars. An empty space was clearly visible. "See those jars? I found one on the floor, and it was broken. We all assumed Meg fell coming downstairs to fetch the jam for breakfast. But the broken jar means she dropped it on her way back to the kitchen."

Brooke's forehead wrinkled. "Do people usually fall going *up* the stairs?"

"Sometimes, I suppose. But if so, she would have been facedown, probably still on the stairs, not the floor." Faith demonstrated Meg's approximate position. "She was lying on her back, exactly as if she had slipped coming down."

Brooke tapped the flashlight against her leg. "I see what you mean." She jerked upright. "Do you think someone pushed her?"

Faith ran a hand through her hair. "I don't know. If it wasn't for the jam—"

"It would look like an accident." Brooke flashed the light toward the far recesses of the cellar. "Let's try to find out more tomorrow. Right now let's look for the passageway to the tower."

"Mrs. Danbury told me no one is allowed in the tower. And that it was dangerous." The woman's lie still rankled. Someone had turned on the lights. Anxiety niggled. *Why did Mrs. Danbury suggest Brooke explore the tunnel?*

"I know. I had to promise I wouldn't go into the tower." Brooke walked into the dark, her beam creating a path. "Probably Ava and

Winslow don't want to be bothered when they're over there, so they tell people it's not safe."

"I doubt that," Faith said. "Winslow's first wife committed suicide by jumping off the tower, remember? I'm sure both of them prefer not to go near the place. I know I would feel that way in their shoes."

"You're right. So who went in there? And why?"

"That is the question of the hour."

As they went deeper into the cellar, Faith focused on her footing. The concrete floor was uneven, and the air had the distinct smell of mold and earth common to underground spaces. Claws skittered somewhere up ahead.

Brooke jumped. "Oh, I hope that's not a mouse."

"Where is that cat when you need him?" Faith didn't see him anywhere. From the dense darkness behind them came a scuffing sound. "Watson?"

No response.

She turned back around, blinking as she tried to see beyond the circle of light. The walls were stone and the ceiling much lower. "How much farther?"

"I have no idea, but it can't be far." Brooke let out an excited cry. "Here we are." She depressed the latch of a door set into the wall. Surprisingly, it opened easily, releasing a blast of even more cold, rank air into the basement. Brooke opened and shut the door partway a couple of times. She leaned forward and sniffed. "Someone's oiled these hinges. I can smell the grease."

Faith felt oddly reluctant to enter the tunnel. "Do you think we should go in there right now? We could wait until tomorrow."

"We'll both be busy. You're not scared, are you?" Brooke's smile was teasing.

"No, not really." What could happen? They'd follow the tunnel to the tower and then turn around and come back. It couldn't be far.

She pictured the grounds in her mind, trying to determine the distance between the house and tower. "All right, let's do it."

Brooke let out a whoop, which echoed in the tunnel. She grinned over her shoulder at Faith. "I feel like I'm in a Nancy Drew mystery. I read every single one of those when I was a kid." She deepened her voice. "*The Secret in the Tower.*"

"Don't laugh. Regina Winterbourne was investigating the death of Winslow's grandmother. She was writing a book about it."

"Did she figure out if that handyman really killed Violet?" The light bobbed as Brooke picked her way along the stone floor. The entire tunnel was stone, with archways at intervals.

"I don't know yet. Ava asked me to read Regina's manuscript."

"Seriously? That's great." Brooke stepped over some stones on the tunnel floor.

Where did those come from? Faith stared up at the ceiling, hoping it wasn't in danger of collapsing. No one would ever find them. With a lurch of fear, she pictured being buried in an avalanche of dirt and rocks.

"There's the door." Brooke played the light over a wooden door trimmed with metal bars and studs. After handing Faith the flashlight, she tried to turn the knob. "It's open."

Alarm shot through Faith. "Don't go inside, okay?" Besides the danger of bumbling around the tower in the dark, she didn't want to breach Ava's trust. And Mrs. Danbury had repeated the prohibition about the tower to Brooke.

Brooke released the knob. "You win. Let's go back and make some hot cocoa." She sidled past Faith in the narrow space. "Last one out is a rotten egg."

She set off, Faith at her heels. Faith was eager to get aboveground again, where she could breathe fresh air and gaze at the stars. A pang of longing shot through her at the thought of being outside, even if it was freezing.

"Did you shut the door?" Brooke asked.

"No, I left it unlatched." Faith distinctly remembered leaving it ajar, wanting the escape hatch left open.

Brooke groaned. "It's shut." She jerked up on the latch and tugged. "And it's locked."

10

"Let me try. Maybe the door is just stuck." Digging in her heels, Faith pulled with all her might, but the door didn't budge. Panic fluttered in her belly. "Someone locked us in."

She remembered the sounds she'd heard behind them in the cellar. Someone must have been following them, so this had to be deliberate. Was Mrs. Danbury responsible? And where was Watson?

"What are we going to do?" Brooke said, her words tense. She pulled out her phone. "No signal, of course, since we're underground."

Faith didn't even have her cell phone. It was upstairs, resting neatly beside her tote in the library. She grabbed her friend's arm. "Wait. Let's go into the tower."

"But you said we shouldn't."

"That was before we were trapped. We can go through the tower, out the front entrance, and back to the house."

"Oh, Faith, you're a genius."

"I don't know about that. But I am crafty sometimes." Relief bubbled in her chest. They were outwitting whoever had played the prank. And most important, they were spared an uncomfortable night in the tunnel. Surely Ava would forgive their going into the tower if she knew the circumstances.

They covered the ground to the tower entrance at a jog, urgency spurring their steps.

"I keep worrying the door is going to be barred at the other end," Brooke said, panting.

"Me too," Faith admitted. She pictured the unknown trickster hurrying to the tower to trap them. "But it was only five minutes ago."

"Is that all it's been? I feel like we've been down here for centuries."

Brooke raced for the door and twisted the knob. "Hooray, we made it!" she yelled when the door opened.

The entrance brought them into the lower level of the tower. They clattered up the stone staircase, eager to reach the front door on the ground floor.

There they received another blow. The massive wooden door to freedom was set with an old-fashioned keyhole—and it was locked, with no key visible on this side of the wall.

"So much for my brilliance," Faith said, deflated. She reached for the light switch, which turned on a hanging chandelier, the kind set with false candles. Perhaps at one point they had been real. "Maybe this will bring someone." She shivered. Like many unheated buildings, the tower felt colder inside than outside.

Brooke checked her phone and sighed. "Still no signal." She glanced around the room, which was perfectly circular, broken only by the staircase continuing up. "Look at the bright side. We're not trapped in that damp, moldy tunnel, and now we have a perfect excuse to look around."

Faith brightened. "True." Although she was squeamish about being in a place where two women had died decades apart, she was curious why someone had been in here recently. She also thought of something else. With all that had happened, she hadn't told Ava about the lights being on the night before when she'd taken a walk in the garden.

The second story was also one big round room, the walls broken at regular intervals by tall windows with diamond panes. In between were bookcases and display cases, but they were empty. Old books with faded covers were stacked in towering piles, and a few pieces of wicker furniture were in disarray, the cushions tipped onto the floor.

"Either the Winterbournes aren't very organized or someone's been ransacking the place," Brooke observed.

"It sure looks that way." Noticing an open window seat, Faith crossed the room to peek inside. Empty. She laughed at herself. "As if that priceless Meissen statue would be in here."

"You think that's what they're searching for?" Brooke asked.

"What else?"

A door creaked open downstairs, and a moment later, a man bellowed, "Hello, are you in here?"

Brooke's expression was exactly like that of a child caught with her hand in the cookie jar, and Faith was sure hers was identical. "I think we're rescued," she said.

Faith switched off the light, and they scrambled down the winding staircase to the main floor.

Winslow Winterbourne stood in the open doorway, frowning.

"Winslow," Faith said, "you're home."

For a moment he looked taken aback. "Yes. I went to New York only for the day. I flew my own plane." His thick brows met over his prominent yet noble nose. "What are you two doing in here?" His voice had the thundering quality of a mythical deity pronouncing judgment.

"We were stuck in the tunnel, so we had to come in here," Faith said. "It wasn't our intention."

"Honestly, it wasn't," Brooke said, her blue eyes round with innocence. "We turned on the lights in hopes someone would come and let us out."

"Who are *you*?" Winslow growled at her.

Faith took Brooke's arm and tugged her forward. "This is Brooke Milner, your new cook. She's a chef at Castleton and very highly regarded by Wolfe Jaxon."

As she'd hoped, the mention of Wolfe and Castleton softened Winslow's demeanor. "I'm glad to meet you. Ava was raving about your skills in the kitchen."

Before he could continue the chewing out that Faith sensed was coming, she said, "Mrs. Danbury told us about the hidden staircases and tunnel, so we were being nosy. I'm sorry."

"Your home is fascinating," Brooke said. "We were comparing it to Castleton. There are hidden rooms and staircases there too, but I think your place has a much more intimate feel."

His gaze around the room held a touch of fondness. "This is an interesting old pile, isn't it? But we don't allow people in here. It's off-limits."

Faith was tempted to mention the night the tower had been illuminated—when he wasn't home—but refrained. "It won't happen again, I promise."

"Come on then. It's cold in here." Winslow gestured for them to step outside. He locked the door with a huge metal key.

"How did you know we were in here? Did you see the lights?" *Or did you lock us in?* Faith reminded herself that she couldn't discount anyone at Wintersea, even the master of the house. Perhaps he had his own reasons for searching the deserted areas of the building and scaring his wife with mysterious happenings.

"The short answer is yes. But it was all due to your cat," Winslow said. "When I got home, he was waiting for me outside the garage. He kept bugging me until I came out back. And then I saw the lights and went to investigate."

As they walked to the house, a familiar black-and-white figure darted out from behind a bush, meowing.

Faith scooped Watson up. His fur was cold. "Did you do that, Rumpy? Did you save us?"

His purr wasn't quite the answer she was seeking, but it was comforting all the same.

Faith's phone chirped just after seven the next morning. She fumbled for it on the nightstand and blinked at the name on the text.

It was from Wolfe. That woke her up, and she quickly scrolled to see his message: *Are you available for lunch with me today at McGinty's? Have things to discuss.*

Faith sat upright in bed. A lunch date with Wolfe was a thrill, even if he only wanted to talk about the blackmail situation. Before she could talk herself out of it, she texted back, *Yes, of course. Let me know the time and I'll be there.*

The reply was immediate. *Noon. I'll be in the back booth.*

That seating arrangement sounded appropriately clandestine for their discussion of Wolfe's problem. McGinty's was dark and discreet too, as befitted an authentic Irish pub renowned for its huge fish sandwiches and corned beef and cabbage.

Faith stretched under the covers, enjoying the feel of the fine sheets. Maybe she could snooze for a few minutes longer. Breakfast wasn't due to be served until eight, and Brooke had told her she didn't need help this morning. She had barely closed her eyes when someone knocked on the door.

"Go away," she muttered, but whoever it was kept knocking. Faith threw back the covers, jostling a disgruntled Watson, and pulled on a robe. "Brooke, is that you?" she called. She couldn't imagine who else would disturb her this early.

No answer.

She opened the door and found Mrs. Danbury holding a tray with a mug of coffee and a cinnamon bun on it. Faith's protests died on her lips. "How thoughtful. Please come in."

Mrs. Danbury ferried in the tray and set it on the nightstand. "I heard you and Brooke had quite the adventure last night."

Surprised by the housekeeper's change in attitude from frosty to friendly, Faith sat on the edge of the bed. "We sure did. Winslow had to rescue us." She reached out and stroked Watson. "My cat helped. If it wasn't for him, we'd probably still be in there." *Huddled together in a corner, freezing, and praying for someone to let us out.*

Mrs. Danbury didn't appear impressed by Watson's marvelous abilities. "Speaking of Mr. Winterbourne, he would like to see you in his office at eight." After telling her where it was, the housekeeper wagged a finger at her. "Don't be late. He's a stickler for punctuality." With that warning, she swept from the room.

A knot formed in Faith's belly as she picked up the bun and took a nibble. One part of her mind knew it was delicious, rich with spices and still warm from the oven, but anxiety turned it into ashes in her mouth.

Was Winslow going to fire her? And if so, what effect would that have on her job—and Brooke's? Marlene wouldn't be pleased if he complained about the behavior of two Castleton employees while their services were on loan.

Faith abandoned the pastry but drank the coffee to sharpen her wits. Then she showered and dressed, choosing heels and a skirt and sweater set. At least she would look professional while getting fired.

Stephanie answered the office door when Faith knocked. "Yes?" She inspected Faith's outfit and made a show of suppressing a derisive smile. Stephanie wore a far more casual pair of wool slacks and a cashmere sweater.

"Mrs. Danbury said Winslow wanted to see me."

"Oh yes. I told her to fetch you." Stephanie smirked. "Come on in." She stood back barely far enough for Faith to get by, then slipped out the door and closed it.

Winslow sat behind a massive desk in the center of the round turret room. He glanced up at Faith over a pair of half-glasses, setting down the pen he was using to mark a bound manuscript. "Have a seat."

Faith perched on the edge of a straight chair in front of the desk, hands folded in her lap and legs crossed at the ankles. She felt like a child called to the principal's office.

He took off the glasses and pushed the manuscript aside, then folded his hands too. "I trust you've recovered from your ordeal?" His smile appeared genuine.

She relaxed slightly. "I have. Thank you. We weren't trapped for long."

"I'm glad to hear it." He picked up the pen and tapped it on the desk. "You're probably wondering why I wanted to see you."

Faith nodded, trying to disguise her nerves.

"I want to plan something special for my wife." He swiveled back and forth, the chair squeaking. "The first day of the conference at Castleton is our anniversary." His distant gaze grew misty. "A year ago we were married in London."

Clearly, she wasn't being fired.

"I'm planning to have a hundred pink roses delivered to our room. We'll be staying in the Jane Austen Suite. Then something extra special for the conference keynote dinner. Coquille Saint Jacques—scallops on the half shell."

That choice will spike the budget.

Winslow must have read her mind because he waved away her unspoken objection. "I'll pick up the tab. Ava will be thrilled."

"Any woman would be," Faith said. "But I'm not the person to discuss these arrangements with. That would be Marlene Russell and our executive chef."

"I know. The domain you so ably manage is the library." He made a small gesture with his hand. "I guess I wanted your input as a woman, what you thought of my ideas."

"I think they're fabulous." Faith's reply was honest, but she longed to add, *She'd probably appreciate you cleaning out Regina's room even more.*

"I'm glad." Winslow wiped his glasses studiously, his face growing somber. "I'm a little worried about Ava. She's been under so much pressure to finish her dissertation. I'm afraid the strain is starting to affect her mind."

Faith's heart lurched at the discussion's change in direction.

"Surely not." She felt foolish, but it was the only neutral remark that came to mind.

He rubbed at his beard with forefinger and thumb. "At first I wrote off her complaints as signs of stress, but lately they've gone beyond that." His tone was grim. "Last night she told me she thinks her life is in danger."

11

Faith's heart pounded. Her suspicions about Meg's accident flashed into her mind. "I know little things have been bothering Ava. But I think I can explain them." *Unless something else happened that I don't know about.*

Winslow's thick brows rose. "How's that? I'm all ears."

"Ava told me she's been hearing mysterious footsteps and voices. I did too when I first arrived—well, the footsteps anyway. I think it was someone nosing around the old servants' quarters over my room." Maybe whoever it was had also been whispering in the hidden corridor. That would explain the voices Ava heard.

Winslow frowned. "There's nothing up there. Just some old furniture and junk. How did you—?"

Before Faith had to confess to more snooping, she said, "Since Ava was already on edge with all the stress over her dissertation, perhaps those harmless sounds took on an ominous cast. Like the way you jump at a strange noise after watching a scary movie." She experienced a pang of guilt, feeling she was somehow betraying Ava. But Cassandra had dismissed Ava's concerns, claiming Ava was overly dramatic. Cassandra was one of Ava's good friends, so wouldn't she know?

"I hope you're right. Ava's gotten it into her head that someone murdered my first wife, Regina." He didn't meet Faith's gaze, pretending great interest in the pen as he spun it on the blotter, his face set in deep lines that made him look a decade older.

Ava must *have been upset to bring up that topic.* Faith had the feeling the subject was taboo around Wintersea despite its obvious existence, like a very large elephant in the room. *A ghost elephant.*

Faith had to bite back laughter at the thought. Ava wasn't the only one with strained nerves.

Faith took a deep breath and said, "I'm so sorry for your loss. I understand Regina was Ava's friend, and she's probably still struggling to get over her death too."

"That's very perceptive. Of course she's grieving. And she may even feel some remorse over the haste of our marriage. But she needn't, as I've told her many times." Winslow spun the chair sideways, his gaze on the drab garden. "If Regina hadn't died, we'd be divorced by now." He swallowed visibly. "She was planning to leave me."

Winslow's confession raises more questions than it answers, Faith mused as she walked back to her room. She'd barely had a chance to react before Stephanie popped into the office with the news that an associate in London was on the line for Winslow. At least that had spared Faith having to come up with something appropriate to say.

Regina died before she could divorce Winslow. Coincidence or not? Had Winslow benefited from her untimely death in some way? Or had he killed her in anger? Faith shook her head, not enjoying the direction her thoughts were headed. Why would he have told her about the pending split if he was guilty of foul play? Surely he would hide his involvement in the role of devastated widower, however false.

Despite her assurances to Winslow that Ava was merely oversensitive, Faith had the nagging intuition that something was indeed rotten in Denmark, as Shakespeare wrote. Or at Wintersea.

Meg, for instance. Had she fallen—or been pushed? When Faith spotted Mrs. Danbury bustling down the upstairs hall, she decided to see what she could find out. She hailed the housekeeper with a wave. "Have you heard how Meg is doing?"

Mrs. Danbury regarded her narrowly. "How nice of you to care. She's out of the hospital and staying at her sister's house in town. She won't be back to work for a while, I'm afraid. In addition to hitting her head, she has a broken rib and a fractured wrist."

"Ouch. I'm so sorry to hear that." Faith hesitated, wondering if she should ask, then decided to plunge ahead. "Do you know what happened?"

Mrs. Danbury looked surprised.

"Something doesn't seem quite right about the whole thing," Faith went on. "She's been up and down those stairs, what? Thousands of times?"

Mrs. Danbury patted her on the shoulder. "You're very sharp, Miss Newberry. Meg told me that she had just reached the top of the stairs when something startled her and she fell." She pressed her lips together. "But she doesn't remember exactly what it was. Head injuries can do that—blank out memory."

"Has she told the police?"

"What good would that do? Law enforcement is no defense against this house." Mrs. Danbury lowered her voice to just above a whisper. "If Wintersea doesn't like you, nothing can help you."

Astonished and more than a little frightened, Faith watched as the housekeeper continued on her way, sensible skirt hardly swaying as she moved silently down the hall.

Once the woman was out of sight, Faith sagged against the nearest wall. She revised her earlier belief that the housekeeper might be an ally. She was as off-balance as others claimed Ava to be.

As Faith straightened up again, her shoulder bumped a painting frame, knocking it askew. When she turned to straighten it, she noticed it was a portrait of Violet Winterbourne as a young woman, or so it was labeled in gold. Dressed in a low-cut gown, a frothy wrap around her shoulders, she held a figurine of Cupid flanked by two women. *The famous missing Meissen?* Violet's serene gaze met hers, innocently unaware of the fate soon to befall her.

"Poor Violet."

Faith jumped at the voice and turned to see Roger standing beside her. She hadn't even heard him coming down the hall.

"What a tragedy." He started walking away, then called over his shoulder, "Going down to breakfast?"

"No. I already ate." Faith fled the rest of the way to her bedroom. She needed some time alone to wrap her mind around the events of the morning. And it was only eight thirty. What other startling events would the day bring?

"Thanks for coming," Wolfe said as Faith approached the rear booth at McGinty's.

"It's nice to be here." Faith unbuttoned her coat and hung it on the peg attached to the booth, a snug enclosure made of dark wood.

The restaurant was packed with patrons enjoying lunch, and a roaring fire crackled in a huge hearth. Buff plaster walls with scenes of Irish castles furthered the illusion that Faith was actually dining in Ireland. That is, except for the American voices at the bar, where several men debated the merits of various ice hockey teams.

Faith was feeling much better than she had earlier in the morning. She had remembered to give Regina's thumb drive back to Ava. She'd wanted to spend the rest of the morning perusing the copy of Regina's manuscript on her laptop, but the professors had kept her busy fetching books.

"I'm having bangers and mash," Wolfe announced, setting the menu aside. "Perfect on such a blustery day."

"It certainly is windy," Faith said, smoothing her hair into place. "I had to fight my way in here from the parking lot." She picked up the menu. *No kidney pie, thank you very much, or corned beef and cabbage. Once a year is enough for that particular dish.* "I'll try the shepherd's pie."

"Good choice."

The server approached and took their orders, which included a pot of tea and glasses of water.

The tea arrived in a brown earthenware pot, and Wolfe poured. "They import this tea straight from Dublin," he said. "I've had the same brand when I was there on business. Good for what ails you, as my nanny used to say."

Faith added a splash of milk and blew on the steaming brew to cool it. When she dared to taste it, she had to agree it was rich and warming. They fell into a comfortable silence as they sipped.

Glancing around at the other patrons, Faith noticed a tall man enter the restaurant and take a seat at the bar. As he unwound the scarf around his neck, Faith realized it was Sean, the Irish professor. It seemed like the guests rarely left Wintersea, so it was almost jolting to see one of them in town.

"So, Faith . . ." Wolfe broke the pleasant quiet. "I've been doing some research."

In the epitome of bad timing, Faith's phone chimed. A text from Brooke: *Where are you?* She turned off the phone with an apology—aloud to Wolfe and silently to Brooke. She'd explain later when she went back to Wintersea. Without mentioning the blackmail, of course, even though she hated keeping secrets from her friend.

"Regarding our, er, little matter, I decided it made sense to begin with the other women on the boat," Wolfe said. "Lulu, Gwen, and Kiesha. They were Valentina's best friends, and as I said earlier, part of the bridal party."

"Are they all models?" Faith asked.

Wolfe leaned back to allow the server to place piping hot plates on the table in front of them. "You might think that, but no." He waited until the waiter left before saying, "Kiesha was a model and still is. Though she's doing mommy ads now, not high fashion. She's in New York. Lulu is a photographer who moved to the wilds of Vermont with her husband and twins." He took a bite of mashed potatoes smothered in gravy and nodded approval. "Gwen went to high school with Valentina. She lives right here in Lighthouse Bay. Her husband, Tim, used to be the second mate on my yacht."

A thrill went through Faith, and it wasn't due to the savory goodness of the shepherd's pie. "Do you think Gwen and Tim wrote the note?"

He deftly cut sausage into perfectly sized pieces. "I agree it's an intriguing coincidence. The note was delivered in an envelope without a postmark, which makes me think it was someone local. Or someone with a local accomplice. So let's take it one step at a time. We need to check them out before making any hasty moves."

We? Faith's heart lifted at being included in his investigation. She would help however she could. "What would you like me to do?"

Wolfe took a healthy bite, chewed, and swallowed. "Gwen owns a gift shop in town called The Swooping Seagull. I thought you could visit and get a read on the situation. See how she's doing, if she seems desperate for money, that kind of thing."

"I'll go after lunch." Faith wasn't sure how she could glean information from the shop owner. She'd have to play it by ear. "I'll also ask my aunt Eileen, without revealing your secret of course. She knows everyone in town, so she's a good resource."

"I trust you," Wolfe said. "You've done an excellent job at the manor."

"Thanks. How kind of you to say so." Despite the praise, disappointment panged, a reaction Faith noticed with rueful amusement. She wanted Wolfe to regard her as a friend, not just an employee. Anything beyond that was something to think about at another time.

"No, I mean it. Even Marlene is impressed."

Faith doubted that very much. The assistant manager watched her like a hawk, eager to pounce on any error or infraction.

"When I asked her how things were going with the library, she couldn't think of a single negative thing to say. That's huge for Marlene." Wolfe chuckled.

Faith smiled. "You know what they say about faint praise."

"I hear you." Wolfe put his hand on the table, close to but not quite touching Faith's. "I also consider you a friend." His eyes crinkled as he grinned. "And I hope you feel the same."

Did he read my mind? Faith scrambled for something to say as she looked around the room. Sean was staring at her, which made her even more self-conscious. "Of course. I'm glad we're friends."

Wolfe let her off the hook by picking up the dessert menu standing on the table. "Hmm. How about a spot of trifle, mate?" he said in an atrocious accent.

Faith laughed. "Blimey, that sounds like it'd hit the spot," she said in her own poor imitation.

After big bowls of trifle—which consisted of ladyfinger cakes, strawberry jam, custard, berries, and whipped cream—Wolfe paid the bill, ignoring Faith's half-hearted objections.

It was nice to be treated to a meal by a handsome . . . friend. She was disappointed when he received a phone call requesting his presence at Castleton Manor and had to oblige.

Before Faith stepped back out into the brisk and windy day, she paused in the restaurant vestibule to search her phone for the gift shop's address. She hoped it would be within walking distance—short walking distance. The weather was distinctly unpleasant for a stroll around town.

Ah, there it is. A block away in an alley off Main Street.

According to the website, it was open. Faith tucked her phone into her pocket and pulled her hat down, steeling herself for the investigation ahead.

"Good afternoon, Faith." Sean came up behind her as she was pushing the door open. He reached around her to hold it for her.

"Hi, Sean. Having lunch in town?" An obvious remark but Faith couldn't think of anything else to say. She'd felt skittish around him ever since she'd witnessed his inappropriate behavior toward Ava in the garden. It was odd how he kept turning up too.

He laughed. "Not a slur on your friend's cooking, I assure you. She's fantastic. I had other business in town."

"So did I. My boss wanted to have lunch." Faith got her bearings and headed up the sidewalk.

Sean fell into step beside her. "Ah, those millionaire bosses. Have to keep them happy." His tone was light, but there was a barb lurking under his words. The usual twinkle in his eyes was missing, and he seemed rather glum.

"It's not like that. Wolfe is quite considerate."

"I'm sure. They all are at first."

Faith wasn't sure what to say to that, so she remained quiet. She hoped Sean would soon veer off to some destination or other. She needed to concentrate on her visit to The Swooping Seagull.

"I'm sorry. That was thoughtless of me. I'm sure he's a fine man. It's not fair to generalize."

Sean's apology surprised her, and she stopped on the sidewalk. "I realize we don't know each other well, but I have the feeling something is bothering you." Perhaps they could address the issue head-on. Faith far preferred that to innuendo.

He laughed. "You are a straight shooter, aren't you? You seem quite chummy with Ava, so I might as well blurt it out. I'm worried about her."

So is her husband. "I know she's been under a strain lately, but won't it get better once her dissertation is finished?"

"Her dissertation? That's the least of her worries." Sean leaned close, his blue eyes boring into hers. "Winslow is going to kill Ava, just as he did Regina."

12

Faith blinked at the Irish professor. "Did you say—?" A strong gust off the water hit her broadside, making her stagger backward. "Ava is in danger from her husband?" Said aloud, her words sounded absurd. "Or so you believe?"

"That's right." Sean hunched his broad shoulders against the wind. "Is there anywhere we can go to talk?"

The Candle House Library was just ahead. "How about the town library? My aunt will let us use her office." Aunt Eileen would be more than happy to help Faith navigate this situation, and Faith needed to ask her about Gwen anyway. The Swooping Seagull could wait a bit longer.

As they turned to walk up the sidewalk, another blast hit Faith square in the back, pushing her forward. "This wind is brutal." In addition to fighting to stay upright, her eyes watered from the cold and her nose was nearly frozen solid.

"Here, let me." Sean held his elbow out to Faith.

She gingerly took his arm, grateful for the support but not quite sure what to make of the man. His pace was brisk, and before Faith could fully catch her breath, they were at the front door of the library.

"After you," he said, opening the door.

Upon entering, the absence of booming, bone-chilling wind was so striking it was like stepping into a vacuum chamber. Faith took a deep breath, her shoulders relaxing in the quiet warmth.

"Faith, what brings you here today?" Eileen bustled around the corner of the desk and greeted her niece with a hug. She touched Faith's cheek with her palm. "You're icy cold."

"It's freezing out there." Faith turned to Sean. "Aunt Eileen, this is Dr. Sean O'Malley, one of the Gothic scholars. He wanted somewhere quiet to meet, and I thought you might let us borrow your office."

"Absolutely." Eileen's eyes were bright with curiosity, but she refrained from asking questions. "Go ahead. Would you like coffee?"

"I'd love a cup," Faith said. She hugged herself, rubbing her upper arms. "I need to warm up after that walk."

"That sounds good. I'll have one too, please," Sean said in his warm brogue.

As he turned toward the coatrack to hang Faith's coat and his own, Eileen fluttered a hand in front of her face, indicating to Faith her favorable impression of the handsome Irishman.

Faith shook her head with a smile. Eileen wasn't hitting the mark with this one. Sean was hung up on Ava Winterbourne.

In the office, Faith settled at the round table in the corner and indicated that Sean should take one of the other chairs.

Eileen carried in a small tray with mugs of coffee, sugar, and creamer and set it on the table. "If there's anything else you need, I'll be right out there at the desk." With a smile for Sean and a significant glance at Faith, Eileen closed the door behind her.

Sean shook a packet of sugar to settle the contents. "Your aunt seems lovely." He tore the top and tipped it into the brew, then stirred.

"She's wonderful," Faith said, pouring cream into her coffee. "It's nice having her nearby."

"I'll bet. I miss my family." He gave a final swirl of the spoon, then tapped it on the rim and placed it on a napkin. With a slight shake of the head, he said, "You must think I've gone round the bend."

She had heard that phrase before. It was British slang for crazy or nuts. "To be honest, I don't know what to think. So please fill me in."

Sean picked up his mug, cradling it in one large hand. "Let me take a step back. I was there when Regina died."

Faith gasped.

"Not on the spot, you understand, but at Wintersea. We all were. Roger, Cassandra, Stephanie, and Winslow. We were celebrating the publication of my first book."

She absorbed that for a moment. "How did Regina seem to you? Was she depressed or upset?"

Sean picked up the spoon and drew lines with it on the napkin. "No, she wasn't. She was excited about some new project of hers. She wouldn't tell any of us the details, but she had that creative glow about her, the one where you're on fire about a project."

"That doesn't sound like someone who would commit suicide." Faith considered and discarded various scenarios. "Unless something awful happened and she acted on impulse."

"That is a very good point." Sean's tone was full of admiration. "But nothing like that went on as far as I know. We were having a grand old time eating, drinking, sailing, swimming—you name it. A wonderful weekend in the sun."

Faith took a deep breath. He was making a case for murder, but every possible angle had to be explored. "It's possible that you weren't privy to her problems. Maybe she hid her depression well. Or got bad news she didn't share."

"You could be right. However, I *was* privy, as you put it, to the fact that Winslow's company was in financial trouble. And Regina was a very wealthy woman in her own right."

Sean's words sank like stones into the quiet air. Outside the office, someone laughed and a book cart rumbled across the floor.

"I suppose Winslow inherited," Faith said quietly.

He nodded.

Another question formed in her mind, growing in urgency until she had to ask, "Is Ava well-off too?"

Again Sean nodded. "She inherited a large estate from her parents. She's a trust fund baby."

Faith's heart plummeted. He was making a convincing case against Winslow, who to all appearances loved his wife. *This* wife. How had he felt about the other? Faith attempted to poke a hole in his premise. "Is there any proof that Winslow was involved?"

Sean gave a bark of laughter. "Of course not. Or else he would have been arrested. The police were convinced she jumped off the tower."

"Take me through what happened, if you remember."

"I'll never forget it. We had dinner on the terrace, then sat around talking and drinking wine. One by one everyone went to bed until only Winslow, Regina, and I were still up. When I left around midnight, Regina said she was heading to the tower to work. She claimed she did her best writing late at night."

So Winslow was the last person to see her alive. "Had they been arguing?"

"No. In fact I remember thinking what a jolly evening it had been. It was the last time we were all truly happy together, without all the snide comments and such you see now."

"It's all very strange." If there had been any evidence of foul play, the police would have investigated further, and they would have suspected her husband first. If Regina *had* been murdered, the perpetrator had committed the perfect crime. Yet as it stood, it appeared that her suicide came out of nowhere.

"Ava and Winslow seem like a very happy couple," Faith said pointedly. Despite the circumstantial evidence, she was beginning to think Sean was seeing what he wanted to see, namely that Ava and Winslow's marriage wasn't good for the woman he loved.

"Of course. Everything is going to look peachy right up until the event, just like with Regina." He shook his head.

According to Winslow, married life hadn't been as wonderful with Regina as it was with Ava. "Do you know if Regina was happy with Winslow?"

His brows rose. "I have no idea. She certainly didn't share the inner workings of her marriage with me." Satisfaction flashed across his features. "But if she wasn't, that only reinforces my theory. Winslow was losing his cash cow, so to speak."

Faith shifted in frustration. "Unless we get Winslow to confess at this late date, we're stuck. Tell me, why are you so concerned about Ava's safety? I have the feeling it's personal."

A frosty silence met her words. Sean pushed back his mug and rose. "I don't care to discuss that, if you don't mind. Thank your aunt for the coffee. I've got to get going."

Faith remained seated after he bolted from the room. She sipped her coffee and thought about the conversation. Sean was eager to float theories of murder but reluctant to reveal his own motivations, which appeared murky. Perhaps he'd made up the story of Winslow's guilt to justify his efforts to break up the marriage.

At least she'd learned something new about the night of Regina's death. Everyone who had been there—except Regina of course—was now gathered at Wintersea. *Interesting.*

After a minute, Eileen popped into the room. "What happened? Dr. O'Malley stormed out of here."

"I hit on a sore subject, I guess." Faith peered at the wall clock. She didn't have time to ask about Gwen if she wanted to get to The Swooping Seagull to snoop. "I'd better go too. I have an errand to run before returning to Wintersea."

"So soon?" Eileen frowned. "If I didn't have a school group coming in, I'd insist you give me an update. It seems like ages since we've talked."

"I know. So much has happened, and I want to fill you in." Had it really been only a couple of days? It felt like centuries had passed.

"How about tonight? I've called a meeting of the Candle House Book Club." Eileen's grin was wicked. "I already spoke to Brooke, and she's coming. She's also been looking for you. What shall I tell her when she calls me again?"

"Tell her . . ." Faith dug out her phone. "Never mind. I'll call her myself."

Maddeningly, Brooke didn't answer, so Faith left a message, telling her she'd be back at Wintersea in an hour or so. With a promise to attend the book club meeting, Faith took leave of Eileen and headed out into the cold.

This time she made it to The Swooping Seagull without interruption. The gift shop was nestled between a toy shop and a candy store in an alley off Main Street. She paused to study the window display, which featured coastal-themed items like lighthouses that lit up, seagull mobiles, lobster buoys, and boxes made of seashells.

A man opened the door and came out, glancing at Faith with curiosity. He wore a knit cap pulled low, making his thick beard and eyebrows more prominent. With a nod, he passed her by on the sidewalk.

She opened the door, and a jingle of bells announced her entrance. The small space was packed with shelves and revolving racks, all crammed with colorful goods. An oil candle burned on the glass counter, wafting the scent of bayberry into the air.

The bead curtains hanging behind the counter parted, and a woman stepped through the opening. She had shoulder-length red hair, a slender figure, and a pouty expression. Glancing at Faith out of the corner of her eye, she shuffled papers on the counter.

"Hi," Faith said. "How are you today?"

The woman's head jerked up. "Okay." A slight smile crossed her lips as she gazed out the front window at the deserted street. "Despite the weather."

Faith examined a display of magnets, pretending great interest. "I hear you. The wind almost blew me off my feet."

"Let me know if you need any help." The woman picked up the phone and placed a call, speaking in a low voice.

So much for that attempt to be friendly. Faith circled the shop, studying dried flower arrangements, wooden lighthouse lamps, and a painting that depicted seagulls circling a lighthouse. Nothing in the store was to her taste, but she tried to find something to buy to account for her browsing time.

While marveling at some truly ugly ceramic ornaments, Faith was overcome with fiendish glee. Since Wolfe had asked her to stop here, she would buy him the silliest item she could find. He liked sailing, so something in that vein would be a good choice. With a mission in mind, searching the shop became more enjoyable, not merely a ploy.

Eventually she discovered something appropriate, a mug relaying a corny witticism about being the "captain of your own destiny." *Perfect.* She nearly giggled out loud.

"Find everything okay?" the clerk asked.

"Sure did." Faith set her selection on the counter and opened her handbag to pull out her wallet, racking her brains about how to start a conversation with this taciturn woman. She glanced around the countertop, looking for something, anything, to remark upon.

Finally Faith spotted a tray of business cards in front of the cash register. They read *Gwen Harrison, Owner*, under the store name. *Harrison.* That rang a bell. She'd met someone named that recently, but who? She shoved the mystery aside for the moment. "Are you Gwen?"

"Yes, I am." The woman's eyes were wary. She took Faith's card and swiped it.

"Nice to meet you. I'm Faith Newberry, librarian at Castleton Manor. I recently moved to town, and I haven't had a chance to get around to all the stores. I love Lighthouse Bay. There's so much to do here." She knew she was babbling, but perhaps something she said would trigger a response.

"It's all right in the summer. Pretty near dead in the winter. I'm not sure why I stay open."

"I've heard that many people with seasonal businesses go south in the winter."

"We don't make enough to be able to do that." Gwen crossed her arms as the credit card machine took its sweet time. "Though my husband would love to buy a charter fishing boat in Florida. It's a year-round season down there."

"Your husband is a captain?"

The sales slip ground its way out of the machine. Gwen ripped it free, then slapped a pen and the slip on the counter. "Tim runs schooner charters and deep-sea fishing. On other people's boats." Her lip curled. "He had a nice fishing boat, but a couple of bad seasons—well, you know the drill."

Faith signed the slip. "That's too bad."

Although Faith hated to hear of people's financial troubles, she knew this was the kind of information Wolfe needed. The couple's financial problems and dreams of Florida provided motive. Gwen hadn't reacted when Faith mentioned her employment at Castleton Manor, so she decided to mention it again.

"You have a great shop. I'll make sure my friends at Castleton Manor know about it." Faith pointed at the mug, which Gwen was wrapping in tissue and placing in a cardboard box. "I bought that for Wolfe Jaxon."

Surprise mingled with alarm flitted over the shopkeeper's face, and her lips parted.

Faith waited eagerly for what she was going to say, but the moment was interrupted when the curtains burst open with a clatter of beads.

Harrison, the employee at Wintersea, stepped into the shop.

13

"Miss Newberry," Harrison said in his deadpan voice, "what are you doing here?"

Faith was startled too. Then she made the connection. Gwen Harrison was married to Tim, the second mate who had once worked for Wolfe, and he must be this Harrison's son.

"I'm buying a gift for my boss." She brandished the box.

"Wolfe Jaxon is her employer," Gwen said, exchanging a significant look with her father-in-law.

"I think I heard that," Harrison said. He examined Faith from head to toe with a frown.

Is he involved with the blackmail? "I'd better get going. See you at Wintersea, Harrison."

"Thank you," Gwen called.

Harrison lifted a hand in farewell.

Faith left the shop in a hurry, anxious to escape the unspoken animosity she'd sensed from the pair. At Wintersea, Harrison blended into the woodwork, not an easy feat considering his sheer physical size. Here, at his daughter-in-law's shop, he was free of those constraints. And she had the distinct impression he didn't care for Wolfe, and by extension, her.

Once inside her SUV, she decided on impulse to swing by Castleton Manor to deliver the gift along with an update. The parking lot was almost empty, but she spotted Wolfe's BMW. Faith parked as close to the house as she could to minimize the walk.

Inside, she headed for the main stairs, noticing that the heat was working again, sending gusts of cozy warmth through the registers.

Although only a few lights were on, the place sparkled with cleanliness. The crew had done an excellent job.

Wolfe's apartment was on the third floor, or more accurately, it was the third floor. Faith rang the bell, hoping she wasn't intruding. Perhaps she should have called first.

"Faith." Wolfe's eyes widened with surprise when he answered the door. "I didn't expect to see you again so soon."

She thrust the box at him. "I brought you a present. And some news."

He took the box, standing back so she could enter. "Thank you. Come on in and warm up. The day's only gotten colder."

In the huge living room with its magnificent ocean view, Wolfe settled her in a chair next to a roaring fire. Papers and a laptop scattered on a nearby sofa revealed he'd been working.

"I get tired of sitting at a desk," he said, gesturing at his papers. "I often prefer to sit out here."

"I don't blame you." Faith gazed out the tall windows. A stormy gray sea was sending foamy breakers toward the shore. Even up here, the sound of waves crashing on the rocks was audible. The effect was almost hypnotic, and as Faith nestled into the warm armchair, she realized how tired she was.

"Do you want coffee or tea?" Wolfe asked. "Or how about hot chocolate? I brought some excellent cocoa back from London."

"Hot chocolate sounds lovely." Faith noticed he still held her gift. "After you open that." She smiled to herself, eager to see his reaction. "I had to buy something as a reason to be in there."

Perching on a chair, he opened the box and unwrapped the tissue, revealing the mug. He held it up and examined it, then grinned. "Thank you."

"Hideous, isn't it?" Faith said. "It was hard work finding the right gift."

"It will look perfect next to the Ming vase. I can't wait to see Mother's face. But first, I'm going to christen it with hot cocoa." He rose, taking the mug to the kitchen.

While Faith waited for him to return, she allowed her mind to empty. The peace that stole over her made her realize how tense and agitated she had been. Not that she minded being in the fray. One of her secret dreads was living a boring life.

That clearly would never happen while she worked at Castleton Manor.

Wolfe came rattling in, carrying a tray with a silver pot, mugs, and spoons. A can of whipped cream, a bowl of tiny marshmallows, and containers of chocolate shavings and peppermint pieces completed the array. "I've made it the way my nanny used to," he said, setting the tray on a low table. "She always made a full pot in case we wanted seconds."

Faith stared at the elegant presentation, contrasting it to the usual microwaved hot water and powdered cocoa. This was much more appetizing. The small girl in Faith thrilled in anticipation.

Wolfe sat on the sofa and filled a mug from the pot. "What do you want on it?"

"Everything," Faith declared.

"The only proper way to have it." Wolfe spooned tiny marshmallows on top of the chocolate, added a tall squirt of whipped cream, and sprinkled that with chocolate and peppermint. "My nanny whipped her own cream, but I'm a slacker in that department."

"No problem." Faith accepted the mug with thanks. "Besides, the canned whipped cream is much lower in calories."

"As if calories are a problem for you," Wolfe said lightly. He doctored his own mug, then clinked it with hers. "To good friends on a cold day."

"To good friends," Faith echoed. The cocoa was delicious—a blend of deep chocolate layered with rich cream and the spark of peppermint. "Yum." She licked a stray dab of cream off her lips with a laugh.

Titan-of-industry Wolfe Jaxon puffed his chest with pride. "Not bad. If I ever get tired of business, I think I'll become a cook."

"Or a nanny," Faith said mischievously. The kindhearted Wolfe would make an excellent teacher of young minds. He had the right blend of patience and humor.

Wolfe screwed up his face in mock dismay. "Horrors!"

They both laughed.

"Let me tell you what I learned." Faith took him through her visit to the shop. "Gwen and her father-in-law definitely reacted to hearing your name. And I'm sorry to say it wasn't in a good way." She hated to have to tell him this.

He pressed his lips together. "Don't worry about it. When you're in my position, a lot of people don't like you. It comes with the territory."

"Do you think Gwen is the one blackmailing you? I could tell she resents how hard it is for her to make a living in Lighthouse Bay."

"Could be." Wolfe took a sip of cocoa. This time he was the one with a whipped cream mustache. "Tim Harrison also owes me money. I gave him a small loan so he could buy a charter fishing boat. After a couple of bad seasons, he sold it, but he didn't pay me back."

Faith was appalled. "And now he wants more money out of you?"

Wolfe shifted uncomfortably in his seat. "I hate to think that of Tim. He was always a good worker. I didn't press him for the money because I knew everyone in town was having a hard time. And I have plenty."

His generosity was impressive, although many no doubt thought he should give away more. They didn't see the hard work that went into creating and maintaining multiple businesses, all of which employed people.

Faith's phone chirped with a text from Brooke. *Have news! Waiting for you to come back.* She reluctantly said to Wolfe, "I'd better return to Wintersea. I wasn't planning to stay away this long. And we have a book club meeting tonight."

Wolfe stood. "Thanks for coming by. Let's keep in touch. I'm sure I'll hear from the blackmailer soon." He laughed ruefully. "It's like waiting for the other shoe to drop."

"Let me know as soon as you do or if you think of anyone else who could be doing this. As far as I'm concerned, the Harrisons are strong suspects."

"It sure looks that way." Wolfe led her to the foyer, where he helped her put on her coat. "Take care." He gave her shoulders a pat, then reached around her to open the door.

As Faith motored down the drive, she glanced longingly in the direction of the gardener's cottage. How she wished she could go there tonight and sit in front of her fire with Watson. Instead she had to go back to Wintersea and into the lion's den. She laughed at herself. Most people would envy her stay at the gorgeous and historic mansion in the company of such illustrious guests.

Maybe including a killer.

The wind was still gusting, and her vehicle was buffeted in the open spots on the road. Once she turned through the gate of Wintersea and reached the shelter of the woods, the air quieted.

As usual, she parked in front of the house. The door opened before she even had the key out of the ignition. Brooke stood in the doorway, her familiar figure outlined by the bright lights in the hall.

"Where have you been?" Brooke cried as she stepped outside. Coatless, she shivered, wrapping her arms around herself for warmth.

"Let's go inside." Faith ushered Brooke into the foyer. "I had to stop by the manor to see Wolfe." As she hoped, that intrigued Brooke enough that she relented in her questioning.

"Ooh, do tell." Brooke gave her a saucy grin. She lowered her voice although they were alone. "I've got lots to share too. Can you come to the kitchen with me?"

"Of course." Faith hung up her coat. Then she remembered her poor cat. He was probably starving. "But I need to feed Watson first."

"I've already fed him. I figured I'd better since I didn't know when you'd be back." Brooke's voice held the merest hint of reproach.

"I'm sorry. I did try to call you." Faith followed Brooke through the house. "And thanks. I appreciate you taking care of Watson for me."

Before they reached the kitchen, the library door burst open. "Faith!" Ava practically danced with delight. "I'm so glad you're back."

Who knew I was so popular?

"I'm going to be on television! A Boston station called today. They want to interview me about my upcoming book."

"That's wonderful," Faith said, genuinely thrilled for her hostess. "When?"

"Tomorrow afternoon." Ava threw a guilty look over her shoulder. "The others aren't pleased. We've got to get the rest of the conference nailed down. But as Winslow said, you have to strike while the iron is hot."

"I agree," Faith said. "Sometimes those doors don't open again."

"That's quite a picture," Brooke said. "Hot irons and open doors."

Ava gave her a strange look.

Faith hastily took her friend's arm. "I'm going to help Brooke in the kitchen. But let's catch up later, okay?"

"Sounds perfect." Ava began to shut the door. "Well, I'd better get back. I just wanted you to hear the news."

"I'm very happy for you." Faith kept a wide smile plastered on her mouth until the door was firmly shut. Then she felt her whole face sag. "Why do I have a bad feeling about that interview?"

"Because you're amazing." Brooke's tone was admiring. "How did you guess she's going to finish Regina's project?"

"What? You're kidding, right?"

Brooke pulled Faith through the swinging door into the kitchen. "Shush. You mean you didn't know?"

"How could I? I've been gone most of the day. I haven't spoken to Ava since yesterday."

"Have a seat." Brooke pointed to a stool. "I need to make the biscuits." After washing her hands, she opened a canister of flour and measured it out.

Faith leaned on the counter, one hand propping up her head, which had begun to ache. "I can't believe this day. It started early, too early, with Winslow calling me to his office to discuss some anniversary surprises for Ava. At first I thought he was going to fire me for going into the tower. Later I talked to Sean at the Candle House Library.

He's convinced that Winslow is plotting to kill Ava like he did his first wife, or so Sean claims."

"The same way?" Brooke measured shortening, using a knife to smooth off the top of the cup.

"No, silly. Don't you think that would be a little obvious?"

Brooke shrugged. "I think it would be a good ploy. Second wife also kills herself by jumping off tower. Bet he'll have trouble finding a third wife though."

Her friend's unexpected wisecrack caught Faith off guard, and a laugh erupted. Brooke joined in, and the two of them giggled until tears poured from their eyes.

"Oh, I needed that," Faith said when the laughter finally died down. She found a stray tea towel and wiped her eyes.

"Me too." Brooke went to the sink to splash water on her red cheeks. She dried off and returned to the biscuits.

Faith watched Brooke deftly cut the shortening into the flour. "You're so good at that."

"I ought to be. When we had the Southern writers' convention I learned how to make biscuits in a hurry."

"You said you had some news for me," Faith reminded her. "And what's this about Ava picking up Regina's book?"

"While you were gone today, Ava recruited me to help her look through Regina's book draft."

Ava must not have been able to wait for Faith to read through the file she'd retrieved from the flash drive.

"And guess what?" Brooke paused dramatically, rolling pin in hand.

"Quit torturing me and spit it out."

"Regina found the missing porcelain figurine. As well as a packet of letters connecting one of Regina's friends to a former servant at Wintersea." She sighed dramatically. "Naturally she didn't say who or which servant."

Faith jumped off the stool. "Do you think it's one of the people staying here? The exact same group was here the night Regina died."

Brooke picked up the biscuit cutter. "That is too strange."

"It's very odd." Faith paced across the floor. "Sean told me they were all here celebrating the release of his book. Winslow was the last one to see Regina alive, according to Sean. That's why he's convinced her husband killed her."

"But why would Winslow do that?" Brooke's forehead crinkled. "What was his motive?"

"Sean said Regina was rich." Faith lowered her voice. "So is Ava. Winslow's company has been struggling. And Winslow told me that Regina was planning to leave him, but I don't know why he would think that."

"Hmm. Money is a prime motivation for murder. But that motive also applies to the figurine. It's worth tens of thousands, Ava said. Maybe someone has been trying to find it."

"Where did Regina say she discovered the figurine and letters?"

"The old nursery. Which is off the hidden corridor upstairs."

Faith yelped with excitement.

"Hold your horses. Regina said she moved them somewhere safe. But she didn't say where."

"That would be too easy, I suppose."

"My thoughts exactly." Brooke moved the cut biscuits to a baking tray. "I think we should check out the nursery anyway. You never know. She could have been lying in case someone else read her manuscript."

Faith returned to her stool. "Ava didn't think of that?"

"No, she got this brainstorm that she should finish Regina's book, and the next thing you know, she was off on a tangent. Evidently Regina was beginning to build a name for herself as a true-crime writer. Ava thinks she might as well take advantage of that ready-made boost to her own career."

"What does Winslow think?"

"I don't believe he knows. He went out this morning and isn't back yet. Ava probably jumped the gun by setting up the TV interview."

Faith considered Winslow's possible reaction to the idea, which would only dredge up Regina's death again. "I agree. Plus, the book's not even finished." Another thought struck Faith. Maybe Regina's death was connected to the mystery Ava was investigating. "And even more important, she could be putting herself in harm's way."

The swinging door flew open and Stephanie marched in, examining every detail of the kitchen. "How's dinner coming, Brooke?"

Brooke slid the tray of biscuits into the oven. "Another fifteen minutes. Once these are done, I'll serve."

"Good. We're all starving. Including Winslow, who just got back." The secretary gave a last look around, then left, her heels clicking on the tile.

"What's her story?" Faith asked. Stephanie always seemed to be lurking, a quiet but watchful presence.

"Ava said she's been with Winslow for years. She was hired as an editorial assistant and promoted to be his right hand. She even helps him select books, according to Ava."

"Interesting. I wonder what she thinks about Ava's new project." Faith moved toward the door. "I'm going to freshen up before dinner and check on Watson. See you in a few."

As Faith reached her room upstairs, she distinctly heard a man and a woman quarreling. She glanced toward the sound at the end of the hall and noticed Ava's bedroom door stood open.

Before she could escape into her room and give the couple privacy, Winslow hurtled into the hall. "This is beyond the pale, Ava!" he yelled over his shoulder. "I won't stand for it!"

14

Faith fumbled with the doorknob, but it naturally wouldn't cooperate.

Winslow strode down the hall, a ferocious scowl on his face.

Ava ran after him. "Winslow, please. I can explain." Then Ava looked at Faith and said, "Tell him it's a good idea."

Faith finally managed to open her door a crack. She stood irresolute, caught between a rock and a hard place. Whom should she try to please, the publisher she happened to agree with or her employer for the week, who was friends with her full-time employer?

She decided to sidestep. "I'm sorry, but I don't know what you're talking about. I've been gone all day." Faith refrained from mentioning that Brooke had spilled the beans.

Winslow stopped next to Faith, arms crossed.

Ava scurried to join them. "I had the most fantastic brainstorm today," she said, slightly breathless. "Brooke and I were reading Regina's manuscript. It's brilliant, and I thought it was such a shame that it will never be published."

"I'll concede that point," Winslow said. "Regina told me it was the best thing she had ever written."

Watson pressed his face against the crack in the door, whiskers sticking through. Faith widened the opening to let him out. He wound his way between her legs, purring, and Faith picked him up. *I missed you too, boy, and I'm sure glad to see you now.*

"She had almost figured out the mystery of who killed Violet," Ava said. "Don't you want to put that tragedy to rest?"

"I thought it was Ralph Briggs, the handyman she fired. He fell or jumped off the cliffs," Winslow said.

Ava put a hand on her husband's arm. "There's more to the story.

According to letters Regina found, another person was involved." Biting her lip, she gave Faith a significant look. "I want to find out who it was. We've asked Eileen to do some background research on the people living in Lighthouse Bay at the time."

She's holding something back. Brooke said someone Regina knew is connected to the old mystery.

Winslow made a humming sound as he stroked his beard. "It is intriguing. I'll give you that. People love it when cold cases are solved."

"Especially when a beautiful woman and a seaside mansion are involved," Ava said. "Can you imagine the cover?"

He nodded. "And it would probably sell incredibly well. My only reservation is that I don't want to dredge up Regina's death." This last was almost whispered. "We were fortunate to keep it out of the tabloids when it happened."

Ava slid her hand through his arm. "Don't worry, dear. We'll downplay that part while giving Regina credit for her work. Don't you see? It will be a wonderful tribute. She deserves that." She leaned against his shoulder.

A moment later, Winslow put his arm around her. Without another word, the pair went off down the hall, heads close together like lovebirds.

"Well, so much for that," Faith told Watson. "I'm so glad I could help." She and Watson pushed through the door into the bedroom.

By the time Faith arrived for dinner, the meal was already under way. Watson had insisted that she make up for her day of absence with excessive cuddles. She slipped into the only empty chair, between Sean and Roger, with a murmured apology. A covered tureen sat waiting in front of her place. She lifted the lid, letting a steamy whiff of beef stew escape.

"Have one of these biscuits," Sean said, passing her the basket. "They're delicious." His usual sparkle was dimmed. Faith thought she detected a haunted look in his eyes.

Next to her, Roger said, "I'll take another. Thanks." He split the biscuit and spread some butter on it, then crammed half of it into his mouth.

"Are you all ready for the conference?" Faith recalled that he was leading a panel on Gothic steampunk as the latest iteration in Gothic literature.

"Hmm? What's that?" Roger apparently hadn't heard her. Like Sean, something appeared to be weighing on him.

"The conference." Faith smiled at him. "You know, that event starting in a few days."

Overhead the chandelier flickered, and gasps and exclamations circled the table. As if in accompaniment, wind howled down the chimney, scattering sparks against the screen.

"Nothing to worry about," Winslow said. "We sometimes lose power when the wind is high."

"I've been telling Winslow we should get a generator," Ava said. "There's a wood furnace as well as the fireplaces, but it can get really cold in here. And it's a pain not having electricity when you're a writer."

"Break out the quills, darling," Sean said, demonstrating with an invisible pen. "That's what the writers of yore did."

"A generator for a house this size would cost a fortune," Winslow said. "We might as well provide power for the whole town. Besides, electrical outages don't happen that often."

Stephanie piped up before Ava could respond. "Speaking of the conference, I finished the agenda for you, Ava. I just need you to make sure it's right before I send it out to be copied."

Ava nodded. "Thanks. I'm so glad to have you take care of the minor details so I can focus on the big stuff." Perhaps she didn't realize how it sounded, but the others did.

Stephanie glared at her boss's wife before ducking her head and concentrating on her stew.

Roger gave a low whistle. "Burn," he whispered.

Oblivious, Ava tapped a knife on a china plate. "Speaking of big stuff, I have something exciting to announce." She glanced at Winslow. "Don't we, dear?"

The others broke into hoots, making Ava wince with seemingly embarrassed pleasure. Faith noticed that despite the wide grins and shouts, there was little true merriment. It all rang hollow.

Ava put up her hands. "Hold on. It's nothing like that. It's about a book. I'm going to finish Regina's last manuscript." She bounced in her chair, barely suppressing a giggle. "It's guaranteed to be a best seller. Right, Winslow?"

Everyone turned to her husband, who said, "It will certainly be our lead title next year."

With a tiny moan, Cassandra clasped her hands at her chest, and Faith remembered her book was due to be published then.

A dense silence fell over the table.

Looking around at each face, Faith was reminded of a tableau in an Old Masters painting, one of those dire Flemish ones. She saw shock, anger, envy, disgust, and even hatred. It was plain that no one liked Ava's plan.

Sean cleared his throat. "I suppose congratulations are in order. Best of luck." His tone conveyed anything but good wishes.

Roger shifted in his seat. Speaking with thinly concealed venom, he said, "What about your dissertation, my dear? Surely that should be your priority. Besides, I always thought Regina's book was cheap sensationalism. Surely that's beneath you as a serious scholar."

Ava's cheeks pinked. "I'm not neglecting my dissertation, I assure you. I'm even thinking that Regina's book, well, *my* book, will help me. What could be more perfect in making my case? I'm writing about a Gothic story that happened in this prime example of the architectural form." She swept her hand in an airy gesture, indicating the opalescent glass, carved woodwork, and roaring fire.

As if on cue, the lights flickered again, causing Faith to stifle a laugh.

If she didn't know better, she'd think Ava was controlling the switch.

This time no one gasped or commented. Emotions tucked away, the other professors projected stony indifference.

"That was perfect timing," Cassandra said once the lights stabilized. She threw her napkin down and rose. "I'd better get back to my keynote speech. Not that it will help if my book is bumped. Good night, all."

Her departure triggered a mass exodus, and Faith made her escape, going to the kitchen to find Brooke. "You won't believe what happened," she said.

Brooke nodded. "I know. I heard the whole thing."

"How? You were in the kitchen." Faith tilted her head. "Do you have the place bugged?"

"No, but that's a good idea. Come look." Brooke opened a door, which led into a butler's pantry lined with stacks of dishes, coffee urns, chafing dish heaters, and the like. At the other end was a pass-through, the sliding window open a crack. "I was eavesdropping in the time-honored tradition of all servants." She hunkered down and peered through the opening. "See?"

Faith bent over and peeked through the narrow space. Ava and Winslow were standing close together beside the fire.

"That didn't go very well," Ava said, rubbing at her eyes. She sniffled. "They aren't happy for me at all."

Winslow handed her a tissue. "Don't worry about it, sweetheart. You know how academics are. They're just jealous."

Winslow might write off their friends' reaction as jealousy, but Sean at least seemed genuinely concerned for her safety. Was Ava putting herself in danger by following in Regina's footsteps? Faith remembered one of the book chapters. Regina had also experienced strange things at Wintersea.

Feeling uncomfortably nosy, Faith stood. "Let's get everything cleaned up. We're going to be late for the book club meeting."

"I hope you don't mind," Brooke said, "but I'd like to take my own car tonight. I need to stop by my place and visit Diva and Bling after the meeting." Diva and Bling were her angelfish.

Faith was horrified. "You didn't leave them alone for the week, did you?"

"Of course not. My neighbor is taking care of them for me. But I'm sure they miss seeing me. No one knows them like I do."

As someone who found a great deal of personality and insight in a feline, Faith held her tongue. Who was she to judge whether or not the angelfish actually knew who Brooke was and missed her company?

After helping Brooke clear the table and load the dishwasher, Faith said goodbye to Watson who was sleeping on the bed in her room. Then she hopped into her SUV and drove to the Candle House Library. *What a day.* She felt like she'd been on the run ever since she woke up.

Wait until Eileen and the others hear our updates. Faith doubted they'd have the time or interest to discuss the book club selection this week once she and Brooke started sharing. *Truth is stranger than fiction indeed.*

To Faith's annoyance, something was going on downtown so she couldn't find a spot in the library lot or nearby. She would have to park a couple of blocks away down a dead-end street and brave a walk in the wind once again. It hadn't subsided—in fact, with the onset of evening it was even stronger than before.

She locked the doors with a beep of the fob and stepped onto the sidewalk. The pale yellow glow of a streetlight was the only illumination, and that was some fifty feet ahead. There were very few houses on this street, and most of them were either dark or had their shades drawn against the frigid night. As a consequence, Faith had to step carefully over the sidewalk, which was broken and heaved due to the severe winters.

Something moved in the shadows behind a garage.

Trees rustling in the wind, no doubt. She shook her head at her nervous reaction and continued walking, her boot heels rapping on the concrete.

Then the crunch of gravel caught her ear, followed by the regular thud of footsteps behind her.

Someone is following me!

15

Faith instinctively walked faster. To her horror, the footsteps kept pace. She dared a glance over her shoulder.

A tall figure was about twenty feet behind her. As it passed under one of the rare streetlights, she saw it was a man, judging by the broad shoulders and style of clothing. The gait was masculine too—long steps without the characteristic hip sway of a woman.

"Sean, is that you?" she called, thinking maybe the Irishman was in town again.

No answer. The figure kept coming.

Should I call for help? Faith scrabbled around in her bag for her phone. Of course it was somewhere in the bottom and kept eluding her grasp. Why hadn't she put it in her coat pocket?

Finally. She pulled it out and promptly dropped it. Wincing, she braced herself for the sound of it shattering, but fortunately it landed on someone's lawn with a soft thud. Panting with fear, Faith reached for it, knowing she was more vulnerable bending down.

But instead of the fast-approaching steps she feared, she heard something so odd she couldn't comprehend the sound at first.

Coarse laughter, all the creepier for its low volume. Next a hoarse whisper that carried clearly. "Mind your own business. This is only a sample." Now the footsteps did speed up—in the opposite direction.

When she ventured to look, she saw him fleeing.

Clasping her phone, Faith set off at a trot, the warm lights of the Candle House Library beckoning. Midge was walking up the front steps. Faith was glad she was back from her conference because she needed a friendly face right now.

"Faith? What's the matter, sugar?" Midge called. Atticus was tucked into her coat, and despite her distress, Faith noticed the Chihuahua wore a knit hat with a pom-pom on top.

Faith stopped, resting her hands on her knees and panting. "A man was stalking me."

"Come on, quick. We'll call the police." Midge ushered Faith inside, still managing to keep a grip on her little dog.

"What's the matter?" Eileen asked in alarm as she rose from her seat by the fire.

"Some no-account scared Faith." Midge gently set Atticus on the floor and took out her phone. "I'm calling 911."

"You really think we should?" Faith asked. "He didn't do anything except laugh at me."

Midge frowned. "He *could* have done something. They need to keep an eye out for the creep."

"Sit down," Eileen said, helping Faith get her coat off and guiding her to a chair.

They sat in silence, Faith absorbing the heat gratefully, until Midge got off the phone.

"Officer Laddy will be right over." Midge pocketed her phone. "How about some hot tea with lots of sugar? That's good for shock." She went to the hot water urn and made Faith a cup.

The front door opened and Brooke entered, bringing a blast of cold night air with her. "Brr. I'm freezing." She noticed the grim expressions on the others. "What happened?"

"A man was bothering Faith," Eileen said.

"What?" Brooke's short hair practically stood on end. "That's awful."

"I had to park a couple of blocks away on that dead-end street," Faith explained. "I heard his footsteps come up behind me. But when I dropped my phone, he just laughed. Then he said—" She had to stop and gulp in some air. "He said, 'Mind your own business. This is only a sample.'"

The women exclaimed in protest.

"What was he talking about?" Eileen asked. "Any idea?"

"If it has to do with Wintersea, then he'll be warning me next," Brooke said. "We're in it up to our necks over there."

A shock ran through Faith. What if the man was Wolfe's blackmailer? After her visit to the gift shop, that was a very real possibility.

Atticus sniffed at her shoes, and Faith bent to stroke his silky head. The pom-pom hat had fallen off. "Do you smell Watson? He stayed home tonight."

The little dog woofed, whether in joy or sorrow, Faith couldn't tell, but it made her smile.

Officer Bryan Laddy showed up in record time, and for once Faith didn't squirm at his relentless efficiency. The young officer was highly intelligent and somewhat intimidating with his tall, slim frame and good looks. He didn't question Faith's veracity. He merely said, "Take it from the top."

After hearing her account of the incident, he asked questions regarding the stalker's appearance, timbre of voice, and length of stride. By the time he was finished, Faith felt confident that he'd eventually find the man.

"That's all I need for now." Officer Laddy stood and scanned each face in turn. "If you see this man again, don't approach him. Call me."

After he took his leave, Brooke sat back in her chair, hand on her chest like a swooning heroine in a novel. "I'd let Bryan Laddy arrest me anytime."

"Keep up your antics and he just might," Midge said in mock reproof. "Now, Faith and Brooke, spill it. I've been dying for your update."

"Where shall we begin?" Faith looked at Brooke.

"How about at the beginning? You start, Faith, and I'll chime in when I show up on the scene." Brooke grinned. "You'll probably need an intermission. And lots of cookies."

She was right. It took an hour for them to relay the full story with all its twists, turns, and snarled threads, long enough for Eileen to make significant progress on her latest knitting project.

"My goodness," Midge said. "I should have been taking notes. Your story reminds me of those convoluted soap operas my granny used to watch."

Eileen's needles flashed and clicked busily. "We're not seeing the whole picture yet." She stopped knitting and held up the length of woven yarn. "See how a pattern is emerging? I follow the directions, but at first I have no idea how it's going to look. It takes a while. I have to trust that it will turn out like the picture."

Her aunt's calm logic soothed Faith. "Let's talk about what we do know." Faith ticked the points off on her fingers. "Meg fell downstairs because someone startled her, according to Mrs. Danbury. Was it deliberate? We don't know. Brooke and I were locked in the tunnel and the tower. That had to be on purpose. And tonight, someone told me to mind my own business."

Brooke took up the narrative. "Strange things are happening to Ava. They also happened to Regina. Regina thought one of her friends was connected to Violet's murder, which she was investigating."

"Now Ava is taking up the case, which could put her in hot water," Faith concluded.

Eileen said, "Let's focus on what we can figure out. Someone needs to visit Meg and see what she can tell us. We can also look into the backgrounds of the people at the house and try to find the connection Regina was talking about."

"Is Meg's last name Kelley?" Midge asked. "If so, then I know her sister, Maeve. She brings her cats to me, and I thought she mentioned having a sister who is a cook."

"I'll find out," Faith said. "Mrs. Danbury told me Meg was going to stay with her sister."

"I'll research the group staying at the house," Eileen said. "Do you have their information, Faith? I can start with their university or book biographies and go from there."

Faith fished around in her tote. "By a stroke of luck I have it right here. I've been lugging around the conference brochure." She removed a booklet and leafed through it. "See? This has the bios of the conference organizers." She handed it to Eileen.

Midge came to look over Eileen's shoulder. "Dr. Sean O'Malley sure is good-looking. I bet his classes are always full."

"He's handsome," Faith agreed. "But in love with Ava."

"Yes, it's really too bad," Brooke said. "I was hoping he would ask Faith out."

The other two women whooped.

"Ava's taken," Midge said. "Maybe you can convince him to look elsewhere, Faith."

But I like— Before Faith could finish that thought, she firmly shut and locked the door. She was happy being single. Wasn't she? "Let's not get distracted. Plenty of time for dates after we finish our investigation."

Brooke smirked at Faith but thankfully dropped the subject. "When do you think you'll have a chance to do the research, Aunt Eileen? We should get together and go over it."

Eileen grew thoughtful. "How about tomorrow afternoon? I have help in here in the morning, so I should be able to dig in then."

"And I'll go visit Meg as soon as I get the chance," Faith volunteered.

Brooke wandered to the snack table. "One more cookie and that's it for me. I still have to swing by my place and visit Diva and Bling."

"They miss her," Faith explained to the others, deadpan.

"Oh yes," Midge said. "There are indications that fish bond with people and recognize faces. I've read all kinds of stories on the subject."

"See?" Brooke did a little dance of triumph as she added milk to her coffee. "They do know me."

"I'm sorry, Brooke," Faith said, contrite. "I'll never make fun of your pets again."

"I forgive you." Brooke picked up a chocolate chip cookie and ate it in two bites, then swallowed the rest of her coffee. "Let's hit the road, Faith. There's no way you're walking by yourself to your car. You know, just in case."

Faith had to admit she was grateful for Brooke's cheerful presence as they walked to her vehicle. This late, the streets of Lighthouse Bay were deserted.

"You really are out in the boondocks," Brooke said when they reached Faith's Honda. She shivered as she glanced at the nearby woods and dark houses.

"Not my first choice of parking area, I admit." Faith unlocked the doors. "Hop in and I'll take you to your car."

Brooke had snagged a place near the library, and Faith stopped next to her red Miata.

"See you back at Wintersea," Brooke said as she climbed out. "Drive carefully."

"You too." Faith pulled ahead and waited until Brooke got the car started and drove away. In weather like this—and with lurkers waiting—one couldn't be too careful.

The drive to Wintersea was uneventful. Faith realized it had become so familiar she could practically navigate the road with her eyes closed. She was yawning by the time she passed through the gate. It had been a long day.

Winding through the woods, her belly tightened in anticipation of the sight of Wintersea. At night, with all the arched windows lit, it resembled a mysterious mansion out of a horror film. But she emerged from the trees and saw nothing but black.

Where is it? The long-threatened power outage must have occurred. She parked in front, hoping she could navigate the stone steps without mishap in the dark. Then she remembered the flashlight she always carried in the glove box, thanks to her father drilling its importance into her head.

She found the flashlight, switched it on, and made it up the front steps without incident. The next hurdle was the door. It was locked.

Faith rang the bell, but she heard no answering peal inside. Of course, it was electric. Now what?

Flashing the light around, she noticed the brass door knocker. She hoped that would be loud enough for someone to hear.

Faith banged the knocker as hard as she could. Again. And a third series of knocks.

At long last the door opened. Mrs. Danbury stood there, holding a lit candle in one hand, peering down at Faith. "Oh, it's you," she said.

"Thank you for coming to the door. Brooke will be along soon, so maybe we should leave it unlocked."

Mrs. Danbury met that suggestion with a look of disdain. "There are candles here in the hall. Take one to light your way to your room."

"Everyone is in bed?" It was only about ten o'clock.

"Under the circumstances, they've all gone up. Except for Mr. Winterbourne, who is loading the wood furnace."

Indeed, delightfully toasty air gusted up through a floor grate and warmed Faith's legs. She struck a match and lit one of the tall candles waiting on the sideboard. Each sat in a holder with a finger loop. Faith felt like a character in a Gothic novel when she picked hers up and climbed the stairs.

Cue the eerie wind that blows out my candle. However, Faith made it to her room without incident. Once inside, she left the door ajar so she could hear Brooke come up. After greeting Watson, who slipped into the hall to stretch his legs, she changed into a flannel nightgown in the bathroom. The nightdress hung to her ankles and had long sleeves and ruffles down the front, very appropriate to the setting, she thought.

"Hey, Watson. How are you, sweet boy?" Brooke's fond murmurings announced her arrival.

Faith went to the door to meet her friend.

"Isn't this creepy?" Brooke whispered. She, too, held a candle. She smiled in appreciation of Faith's nightgown. "Your outfit is perfect."

"That's what I thought." Faith followed Brooke to her room across the hall.

This room was lovely, decorated in lavender with lots of ruffles. It didn't have the advantage of an ocean view, like Faith's room, but the vista of woods and gardens was probably very pleasant in the daytime. Tonight of course, there was only inky black beyond the windows. Brooke closed the curtains.

"Not having electricity makes me realize how dependent we are on it," Faith said. "Even if you have a book to read, it's not that easy by candlelight. We're so lucky Castleton has a generator." The power there went out for only a minute, if that.

Brooke walked into the bathroom and turned on the tap. "We still have a little hot water, probably from before the outage," she called. "I'm going to take advantage of that and wash up."

"I'll leave you be then," Faith said. "Come on, Watson."

Instead he jumped on Brooke's bed and curled up.

Faith called him again, but he wouldn't budge. The next step was removing him bodily, but she hated to force him against his will.

Brooke stuck her head out of the bathroom, washcloth in hand. "What's going on?"

Faith pointed at Watson. "I think you have an overnight guest. I guess he's tired of being in my room."

"He can sleep with me. I don't mind."

"All right. If you're sure. Good night, Brooke, Rumpy."

Brooke called good night, but Watson only purred. The traitor.

Back in her room, Faith picked up the candle and took it into the bathroom, where she washed up and brushed her teeth by candlelight. It was novel now but how limiting it must have been in days past.

She carried the candle back to the bedroom and set it on the nightstand. The edition of Gothic short stories she'd found downstairs was waiting, and she opened it with a sense of pleasure. After a hectic day, nothing soothed her as much as reading a good book. But as she'd told Brooke, reading by the flickering and rather dim glow was difficult. She managed only one story before she had to set the book aside because her eyes were so tired.

Faith blew out the candle and snuggled under the covers. The house was dead quiet, the howling wind the only sound. She missed Watson and for a moment considered retrieving him from Brooke's room. But then that thought vaporized and she slept.

Until something touched her face.

16

Faith screamed and launched herself away from the clammy touch to the other side of the bed. She scrambled to an upright position, groping for the light switch. She hit the lamp, and it fell over with a crash.

A dark shape stood next to her bed, swaying.

She screamed again, waves of panic washing over her.

A light appeared in the hallway. "What is it? Faith, are you okay?" Brooke burst into the room, waving a flashlight, Watson at her heels.

When the beam hit the figure, it revealed Ava Winterbourne, staring straight ahead with a fixed gaze. She mumbled unintelligible words and appeared unsteady on her feet.

Faith huddled in the bed, shaking. "She touched my face. And it scared me." Her teeth began to chatter, and she had to bite down to stop them.

Watson jumped onto the bed and ran to her.

Doors up and down the hall opened, and the murmuring of voices was heard.

Winslow, wearing a robe over pajamas, reached them first. "What's going on in here?"

"Your wife is sleepwalking," Brooke said. She pointed the flashlight at her.

Ava turned and shuffled toward the bathroom. Faith noticed her feet were bare.

"Is everyone all right?" Sean popped his head through the doorway. "I heard screams."

The others crowded behind him in the hall.

"That was me," Faith said. She put a hand to her chest. Her heart was still racing.

Watson nudged her arm with his head, and she stroked his soft fur. He crawled into her lap, purring.

"I'm very sorry about this, Faith," Winslow said. He had an arm around his wife's shoulders and was guiding her toward the door. "She does this sometimes when she's under stress."

Sean stood aside when Winslow reached the doorway. "Need any help?"

"No. We're fine." Out in the hall, Winslow told the others, "Excitement's over. Everyone can go back to bed."

The sounds of muttering and doors shutting followed.

"I'll be off then," Sean said to Brooke and Faith. He wiggled the doorknob. "I'd lock this if I were you." He disappeared down the hall.

"No kidding," Faith said, then scolded herself for forgetting to lock the door. "I'll remember that from now on." She gently moved Watson off her lap so she could get up.

"There's a bolt," Brooke said, helpfully sliding it back and forth. "You could use it. Though I doubt she'll be back."

"Maybe she'll visit you next." Faith shook her head, attempting a laugh. "My goodness, I thought I was going to have a heart attack."

Brooke shuddered. "Fingers touching your face while you sleep—it sounds like something out of a horror film."

"Really. Thank goodness it was just Ava. Let's try to get some sleep. Good night." As soon as her friend was out of the room, Faith locked both the knob and the bolt. Then she double-checked that the chest was still blocking the other door.

Watson curled snugly into her side once she got settled in bed, and thanks to his warm comfort, Faith soon drifted off again.

She awoke to an extra bright morning, thanks to the lights that had been left on during the power outage. "I'll take it," she said, switching off the bedside lamp. The one on the other side of the bed was on the floor where she'd pushed it by accident. Fortunately it wasn't broken.

When Faith opened the curtains, she saw that the day was overcast and still windy. Rain ticked against the glass. For a fanciful moment, she wondered if the weather was always gloomy around Wintersea, if it was enclosed in its own weather system.

Still in need of solace after the frightening episodes last night—the stalker and the sleepwalker—Faith ran a hot bubble bath. She pinned up her hair and climbed in, exhaling as the steamy water enveloped her. Then she reached for a fashion magazine. *Who needs to read scary Gothic stories when you're living one?*

Watson leaped onto the toilet seat and began to wash, one of his rituals while she bathed. It always made her smile.

She soaked and read, turning on the tap whenever the water cooled. A clock on the bathroom wall informed her that breakfast would be served shortly. Faith had offered to help Brooke cook, but Brooke had brushed her off, saying she was all set. *The least I can do is show up to eat it on time.*

After her bath, Faith continued the theme of cozy comfort and selected a thick knit turtleneck and a pair of warm dress pants to wear.

Watson insisted on going downstairs, and Faith didn't have the heart to stop him. He'd been left in the room all day yesterday, and that wasn't fair.

At the front door, he meowed insistently.

"Don't go far, Watson." She shivered as she let him out. "It's nasty out there."

In the dining room, an exhausted-looking Ava sat with a mug cradled in her hands. She was the only one in the room. "I'm really sorry about last night. I heard I was sleepwalking again."

"You don't remember it?" Faith asked. She went to the buffet table and spooned scrambled eggs onto a plate. Brooke had also made bacon and sausage links. She took some of each.

"No, I never remember anything." She attempted a chuckle. "One time I went outside. My roommate found me wandering down the sidewalk."

"That sounds dangerous." Faith selected wheat toast and then moved along to the beverages. She needed coffee and lots of it today.

Ava yawned. "We have to make sure the front door is locked with a dead bolt key to keep me inside."

Faith sat down with her breakfast. "When's the interview?"

"This afternoon." Ava yawned again. "I'm sorry. I'd better take a nap. I was up early this morning writing notes." Her lips turned up briefly. "I want to entice without giving everything away."

Faith chewed a bite of fluffy eggs, detecting a hint of cheese. After swallowing, she said, "That should be easy. We—I mean, you don't know everything yet, so you can't give it away."

"True. I have to finish the investigation Regina started. Otherwise I won't really have a book."

There was her opening. Choosing her words carefully, Faith asked, "Do you think it's safe to investigate? What if Regina's death was connected to something she learned?"

"How can that be? Violet Winterbourne died decades ago. Who cares about that now? It's merely an intriguing cold case."

Faith hoped Ava was right, but until they found out the rest of the story, she preferred to operate with caution—an approach the writer and historian obviously didn't favor.

Before Faith could say anything further, Roger and Cassandra entered the dining room, Roger eyeing them both with a smirk. "Sleep well?" he asked, his tone suggesting the opposite.

"Oh yes," Faith said, not wanting to play into his hands. She reached for the jam holder, pausing when she saw one of the containers held raspberry that looked like the jam Meg had been retrieving just before her accident. She turned to Ava. "I've been thinking about poor Meg. I'd like to bring her some flowers. Do you have the address where she's staying?"

"I sure do. With her sister, Maeve Kelley, on Harbor Street. Do you know where that is?"

Faith pictured the layout of Lighthouse Bay. "I think so. Is it near Main Street?"

"That's right," Cassandra said. "I used to have an apartment on Harbor." She and Roger sat at the table with their food.

"I didn't know you lived in Lighthouse Bay," Roger said. "I thought you were a Boston native."

"I'm a city girl," Cassandra said, "but I spent several summers here on the Cape while I was in college."

"I'll give you Maeve's number after breakfast, Faith," Ava said. "I already sent flowers, but I'm sure more will be welcome. Meg loves tulips, by the way."

"Perhaps I'll go over today if she's up to it. And if you don't need me."

"I would like your help this morning to get ready for the interview. Then I plan to lie down for a while. The crew will be here at four. I'd love to have you on-site when they come."

"Of course. I'll go after lunch for an hour or so."

"You must be excited, Ava," Cassandra said, her expression openly envious. "Being interviewed on television about your work is a thrill."

"I'm sure you'll have an opportunity soon." Ava's smile was kind. "Your book is groundbreaking."

Cassandra ducked her head but not quickly enough to hide a look of fury. She picked up a piece of toast and took a savage bite.

"Don't be patronizing, Ava," Roger said lightly. "You're in the ascendant now. But remember, fame and fortune are fickle."

Ava shot him a glare that could have peeled paint.

Sean sauntered into the room. "Good morning, all. I'd say it's a lovely day, but it isn't." He picked up the tongs and grabbed a sausage. "Was that Winslow I saw speeding away? I thought surely he'd be here for your television debut, Ava."

She thrust out her lip. "He had to go to Boston for a very important meeting that's been scheduled for weeks. With his banker, I think. Something about a line of credit." She put a hand to her mouth, clearly stricken by this indiscreet remark about her husband's business.

With a sly smile, Cassandra elbowed Roger, who pretended great interest in stirring his coffee.

As for Faith, she was reminded of what Sean had said about Ava and Regina both being wealthy. Was Winslow running short of cash again?

Sean sat at the table and pulled his chair in, then flicked a napkin open. "Don't worry. We'll be here for you. You can count on us."

"Yes, we'll all be cheering you on," Cassandra said. Her eyes didn't quite echo her words.

"Where's Stephanie?" Ava asked, craning her neck to peer out the doorway. "She's usually down by now."

"I'm pretty sure I saw her in the car with Winslow when he left, darling," Sean told her.

Interesting that Winslow would take his assistant on a sensitive errand like that, Faith mused.

After breakfast, Faith hung around to help Brooke clean up. "The meal was delicious," she told her friend, "but it's a wonder I don't have indigestion. The tension was so thick you could have cut it with a knife. All the subtle sniping was driving me crazy."

"Did you learn anything?" Brooke stacked used dishes on a tray.

Faith gave her a summary of the conversation as she gathered silverware. "I'm due upstairs to help Ava soon. Do you want to come with me? Maybe we can check out the nursery. Just to dot the i's and cross the t's."

"Let's get these dishes loaded in the dishwasher and we'll go up."

Ten minutes later, as they reached the top of the stairs, shrieks and moans were clearly audible from Ava's room. Faith and Brooke exchanged glances and broke into a run.

Faith halted at the door, causing Brooke to bump into her. The bedroom appeared as if it had been ransacked. The bedcovers were flung off, books lay splayed all over the carpet, and the closet door stood open, most of the contents drooping off hangers or puddled on the floor.

Ava rooted frantically through her bureau, tossing things left and right. Socks here, T-shirts there. She paused in her search. "Where are they? Where did I leave them?" She put both hands in her hair and tugged.

"What's going on?" Faith stepped cautiously into the room.

Ava burst into tears. "My notes. They're gone."

"Notes for what?" Brooke asked. "Maybe we can help you find them."

"For the show," Ava said. Her voice rose to a wail. "I'm doomed. I'm going to make a huge fool out of myself."

She's misplaced something again? Faith almost found Ava's over-the-top display amusing, the way she did toddlers having tantrums, but she also sympathized. It was frustrating to lose something important, especially when that loss could lead to public humiliation and failure. She was certain of one thing: panicking wasn't going to help.

"Ava, stop for a minute," she urged. "Take a deep breath."

"In and out, in and out," Brooke said, demonstrating. "It really helps when I start freaking out in the kitchen."

The suggestion to breathe seemed to pass Ava by, but surprisingly she fastened on Brooke's comment about her job. "You get stressed out cooking? I always thought it would be such a fun, relaxing career."

Brooke hooted. "Relaxing? Girlfriend, you haven't *seen* stress until you work in a kitchen during a rush. It's obviously as hot as an oven, and you have to move at top speed while producing perfect food. Usually with the head chef yelling at you to hurry and the other cooks getting in your way."

"Wow. Hats off." Finally calm thanks to Brooke's skillful diversion, Ava said, "I'm looking for a purple manila folder. I'm pretty sure it was here when I went down to breakfast. Now it's nowhere to be found."

Faith gazed around at the shambles. "I'll take your word for it. Did you go anywhere else this morning? Maybe you carried it with you somewhere by accident."

"I don't think so, but we can retrace my steps." Ava led Faith and

Brooke through the hall and downstairs to the dining room. "You didn't see it when you cleared up after breakfast, did you?"

"No, I didn't," Brooke said. "If I had, I would have left it on the table or the sideboard."

Ava sighed. "I guess I'd better get to work and try to re-create my notes. First I'm going to Regina's room. She had some books up there I want to use. Would you like to come?"

Behind Ava's back, Brooke nodded vigorously.

"Sure, we'll tag along," Faith said. "I might have ideas for other books that will be useful."

"Come on then," Ava said. "Let's go. Four o'clock is coming fast."

Like Faith had been before, Brooke appeared both fascinated and appalled when she entered the dead woman's bedroom. "I feel like I'm in a creepy novel," she whispered to Faith. "This place is a time warp."

Faith nodded but put a finger to her lips. Fortunately Ava appeared not to overhear. She was busy searching through the packed bookshelves. Faith went to her side to help while Brooke wandered around.

Ava was showing Faith a guide to valuable porcelain when Brooke yelped.

Faith whirled and gasped when she saw what Brooke held.

A purple manila folder.

Brooke waved it in the air. "Is this what you were looking for?"

Ava thrust the guidebook at Faith and ran to Brooke. She snatched the folder and opened it up. "Yes, it is. Thank you." She hugged the folder to her chest, then flipped it open and riffled the pages. "Thank you so much. You've saved my life." Her expression shifted from relief to confusion. "How did it get in here?"

"Didn't you bring it in here?" Brooke asked.

"No, I haven't come in here today." Ava's brow creased. "At least I don't think I did. Wouldn't I remember?"

Faith said, "Maybe you were deep in thought. I do that all the time. I'll move something when my mind is focused on something else, and later I have no recollection of where I put it. Sometimes I think I'd leave my head behind if it wasn't attached."

"Maybe you brought it in here when you were sleepwalking," Brooke suggested.

"No, I know I had the folder this morning." Ava screwed up her face. "I think."

Faith and Brooke exchanged looks of concern.

Still hugging her notes, Ava twisted back and forth. "I don't know how much more of this I can take." Her gaze skittered around the room. "It's this house. I never lose things when I'm somewhere else. We went on a trip to New York for two weeks, and everything was perfect."

Brooke, in her practical way, asked, "Did you leave the key to this room in your bedroom this morning?"

Ava stopped moving and pulled a key out of her pocket. "I did. It was in my dresser drawer, where I always leave it. I just picked it up when we were in there a couple minutes ago."

"And your door was unlocked," Brooke said.

Ava gaped at her. "You think someone took this folder from my room and put it in here?"

"Someone did," Faith said. "You or someone else. If the key was in your room, they could easily have borrowed it while you were at breakfast."

Ava pressed her lips into a grim line. "I don't know what's worse— thinking I'm going crazy or having someone try to send me there."

17

"Boy, Ava's in a tough spot," Brooke said, pulling the tin of freshly baked cookies out of the back seat. "Who do you think is tormenting her, if that's what's going on?"

"I have no idea. Or rather, lots of ideas but nothing definitive." Faith grabbed the bouquet of red tulips she had bought for Meg.

The duo was parked outside Maeve Kelley's neat white bungalow on Harbor Street. Ava had decided to focus on studying her notes before lunch to calm her nerves, so they'd come over earlier than Faith had planned.

Brooke shut the car door. "Hey, there's a police cruiser parked over there."

Uneasiness trickled down Faith's spine. "I hope it's nothing to do with Meg."

"Why would it be? She's doing better, right?"

They walked up the brick path. When they reached the front porch, the door opened and Bryan Laddy emerged.

"Officer Laddy," Brooke said, "what are you doing here?"

He adjusted his hat, a gesture of greeting. "I really can't discuss it. Police business."

"Meg's all right, isn't she?" Faith asked.

Laddy cocked his head. "She's fine." He studied the tulips and the tin Brooke carried. "Bringing gifts? That's nice, ladies. Have a good day." He strode off, every inch the heroic lawman.

"As Midge would say," Brooke whispered, "be still my beating heart."

"Enough pining over handsome policemen. Let's find out why he was here." Faith shifted the bouquet in her arms and rang the bell.

A short, round woman who resembled Meg answered the door.

"Good morning. How can I help you, lass?" Like her sister, she had a soft accent.

Faith explained who they were. "We'd love to see Meg if she's up to it," she concluded.

"Oh, she'd love to see you. That officer got her riled up for certain." Maeve opened the door wide. "Come on in and make yourselves at home."

Immediately upon entering, Faith felt enclosed by cozy warmth. The carpet was thick, the woodwork polished with lemon oil, judging by the faint scent, and lace curtains and flowered chintz were everywhere. Faith and Brooke set their gifts on a hall table, then took off their coats.

"Would you like a cup of tea?" Maeve said. "I've just got the kettle on."

"Yes, please," Faith said, and Brooke nodded beside her. They picked up the flowers and the tin of cookies again.

"Meg's in the family room. This way." Maeve bustled down the short hall, passing a formal living room, going through a dining room, and entering the kitchen.

Beyond the kitchen was a large room across the entire back of the house. Sliding glass doors provided a view of a patio hung with bird feeders. Meg sat in a recliner watching the birds. The cook wore a bandage on her head, and her wrist was in a cast.

"Hi, Meg, it's Faith Newberry. Do you remember me?"

Meg's face lit up. "Of course I do." She noticed the flowers Faith held. "Are those for me? How thoughtful."

"Shall I set them here?" Faith placed them on a nearby table where Meg could easily see them.

"Perfect." Her bright gaze turned to Brooke, and she smiled.

"I'm Brooke Milner. I brought you cookies." She set the tin beside the tulips. "From one cook to another."

"Brooke is pinch-hitting at Wintersea," Faith said. "She usually works at Castleton Manor with me."

"Castleton Manor. What a lovely place. Have a seat, won't you?"

Faith and Brooke selected armchairs.

"How are you feeling, Meg?" Faith asked.

Meg grimaced. "A lot better." She held up her hand. "But it will be a while before I use this hand to whip cream or cut vegetables."

"I'm telling her she needs to retire," Maeve called from the kitchen. "Or if not, she shouldn't go back to Wintersea."

"Why's that?" Faith asked. "Does it have something to do with why Officer Laddy was here?"

The kettle whistled, and Maeve picked it up. "Hold on a minute. I'll be right there, and we can talk."

The trio sat quietly, gazing out the picture window and listening to the comforting sounds of Maeve getting their tea in the kitchen. Faith spotted chickadees, goldfinches, wrens, and a male cardinal darting around the feeders.

"Here we are," Maeve said, puffing as she lugged a heavy tray into the room. She set it on the low table. "I've added some nibbles." Her idea of nibbles included a tiered tray of tiny sandwiches, pickles, and chips. "Help yourselves."

"I can see the cooking talent in your family goes beyond Meg," Faith said.

Maeve shrugged, but Faith could tell she was pleased. "I'm not a patch on my sister, but I try." She poured a cup of tea and handed it to Faith.

Brooke piled food onto a small plate. "What are these?" She peered inside one sandwich, then took a bite. "Yum. I'll have to try making them."

"Ham, brie, and apple." Maeve bristled with pride. Having served her guests, she carried a cup of tea to Meg, placing it near her uninjured hand. "There you are, love."

A minute later they were all settled, sipping and munching.

Maeve broke the silence. "Wintersea is not a good place. My sister was pushed down the stairs."

Faith jerked her hand, splashing tea onto her lap. "Someone pushed you?" Although Faith had suspected there was something wrong about Meg's accident, hearing it out loud was alarming.

"Is that why Officer Laddy was here?" Brooke asked.

"Yes, but fat lot of good it did." Maeve frowned. "He said he doesn't have enough to investigate, let alone bring charges."

"Tell us what happened," Faith said.

Meg set her teacup down, her eyes distant. "I woke up in the hospital with a headache, and at first I didn't remember what happened. But it's been coming back to me in bits and pieces."

"That's why Laddy is discrediting it," Maeve said. "He thinks she might be filling in the blanks herself. Not on purpose, mind you, but that's what the brain does sometimes."

"I don't think I am," Meg said. "That morning I went down to the cellar to fetch a jar of jam, something I've done a million times. I was at the top of the stairs when I heard something in the cellar. I turned around to see what it was. Next thing I know, I feel a shove and I'm flying down the stairs. Then nothing."

"That's horrible," Brooke said.

"You didn't see who pushed you?" Faith asked. "How about odor, like perfume? Or a voice?"

"No, none of that." Meg's face creased in thought. "I've been over it a thousand times."

"The sound you heard. What was it like?" Brooke asked.

"A squeaking sound. Like metal."

"When we're back at Wintersea, we'll go down to the cellar and try to figure out what that was," Faith said.

"That's nice of you, but I don't know what good it will do." Meg's expression was bleak. "I did love that job, cooking for Ava and Winslow. But I don't know if I can go back, not knowing who pushed me."

Faith reached for a sandwich, stalling to take advantage of this opportunity. "You've been there a long time?"

Meg nodded. "I came on board when Winslow married Regina. She was so busy with her writing that she needed someone to cook for them. Plus, they had lots of parties. Maeve used to help with those. Still does once in a while."

Faith's heart began to beat a little faster. Meg and Maeve were independent witnesses to events at Wintersea. "Were you there the night . . . ?" She hesitated. In for a penny, in for a pound, as the saying went. She cleared her throat and pushed on. "The night Regina died?"

The sisters exchanged glances, communicating something silently.

"We were," Meg said. "Though not there when it happened, understand. I didn't live there then, so we'd cleaned up and gone home."

"I don't believe she killed herself." Maeve's voice was surprisingly loud in the snug room. "She was full of life, excited to be working on her book, and so in love with her husband."

The comment took Faith by surprise. "Do you have any idea why Winslow might have thought Regina was going to leave him?"

Maeve shook her head. "I'll never believe it. She loved him, and he loved her."

Meg looked thoughtful. "Did Winslow tell you that? I feel terrible not saying anything to him, if he's been living with that wrong assumption."

"What do you mean?" Faith prodded.

"Regina confided in me over tea in the kitchen not long before she died that she was planning a surprise trip to Tuscany for the two of them. To cheer him up because his business wasn't doing well. That didn't matter to her one whit. 'I have plenty of money for the both of us,' she said."

Poor Winslow. He must have gotten wind of her plans and interpreted them incorrectly.

"Meg, do you think Regina killed herself?" Faith asked gently.

"I agree with Maeve. I was shocked when I got the call." Meg raised a shaking hand to her mouth, eyes bleak with remembrance. "Wintersea was a sad place after that, I tell you. But I had to stay on for Winslow. He was helpless. The man can't boil water. I don't know what he did before Regina."

Faith remembered the housekeeper. Where did she fit in? "Tell us about Mrs. Danbury. I get the impression she was very devoted to Regina."

Again the sisters shared a look.

Meg inhaled. "Florabelle Danbury is an interesting woman."

"Florabelle?" Brooke sputtered. "That's her name? I've never seen a less flowery person."

"I know," Maeve said. "You wonder what her mother was thinking."

"Her sister's name is equally over the top," Meg said. "Azalea."

The women burst into laughter.

"I'm sorry," Faith said, "but that is really awful."

"At least they didn't pass the madness to a new generation," Meg said. "Azalea named her daughter Stephanie."

Stephanie? "Don't tell me Winslow's secretary is Mrs. Danbury's niece," Faith said.

"That's right," Meg said. "Mrs. Danbury got Stephanie the job at Winterbourne Press after she graduated from college."

"You'd never guess it," Brooke said. "They look nothing alike."

"Stephanie takes after her father. In more ways than one." Meg bit her lip. "Sorry. I shouldn't gossip."

Please gossip! Faith wanted to hear more about the mysterious secretary.

"What's a harmless natter between friends?" Maeve asked. "Stephanie is bright, ambitious, and a tiny bit ruthless."

Meg snorted gently. "That's a perfect description. I thought when Regina died Stephanie would finally get her way with Winslow. But he went and married Ava."

Faith was puzzled. "Stephanie is in love with Winslow?"

"As much as a woman like that can be in love," Maeve put in. "Stephanie is all about number one."

"That was an interesting visit," Brooke said as they drove away from Maeve's house. "They're nice ladies too. I enjoyed meeting them both."

Faith was still mulling over the surprising revelation that Mrs. Danbury and Stephanie were related—and that Stephanie had hoped to marry Winslow. "I wonder if Stephanie's behind the strange incidents that Ava's experiencing. Misplacing things, hearing weird noises . . ."

"To get back at her for marrying Winslow, you mean?" Brooke looked thoughtful. "I can see that. The occurrences are petty but annoying."

"Ava has a pretty dramatic personality. It's probably easy to push her buttons." Faith pictured Stephanie secretly laughing at her boss's hapless wife.

"You could be right. The only thing is, Meg's accident wasn't harmless. She was seriously hurt and seems to be thinking of resigning her post. And locking us in the tunnel was dangerous. We could have been stuck down there or in the tower all night. We could have died of exposure before anyone found us."

Faith revised her theories. "True. Could there be two people pulling stunts?"

"Either that or we're not seeing the whole picture."

For the rest of the trip to Wintersea, they rode in silence.

As they pulled through the gate, Brooke said, "We never visited the nursery. Even if the figurine isn't there, I'd still like to see the place. Maybe we'll find a clue Regina left behind."

"Good idea. We'll have a couple of hours before the television crew arrives."

Mrs. Danbury entered the hall as they walked in, ready to take their coats.

The sight of her reminded Faith of her hostile encounter with Harrison the previous afternoon. Maybe Mrs. Danbury knew something. As Faith handed her coat to the housekeeper, she remarked in what she hoped was a casual tone, "I haven't seen Harrison this morning. Is he all right?"

"All right? Whatever do you mean?" Mrs. Danbury hung up Faith's coat and snatched Brooke's from her hand.

Faith always seemed to step wrong with this prickly woman. "Nothing. I thought he might be sick or something." *And by "or something" I mean engaged in blackmail.*

"He took the day off, that's all." Finished with the outer garments, Mrs. Danbury smoothed her spotless clothes with both hands. "Is there anything else I can do for you?"

"Not a thing. Do you need anything, Brooke?"

The grandfather clock on the landing bonged.

Brooke looked at it and squeaked, "I need to make lunch." She rushed off toward the kitchen.

Left alone with the housekeeper, Faith said on impulse, "That was a nice thing you did, getting your niece a job with Winslow. She seems to love it."

A covert smile slid across Mrs. Danbury's face. "That's what you do for family. You help them get what they want."

Faith shivered. Why did such a benevolent sentiment sound so ominous?

18

"Mrs. Danbury's a crackpot," Brooke said after lunch as they climbed the hidden staircase used by the servants, accompanied by Watson. "She probably gets a rise out of scaring people, just like her niece."

"Maybe so," Faith said. But try as she might, she couldn't shake a feeling of dread. All week she'd sensed things were escalating, although on the surface not much appeared to be happening. *Is this what Ava feels—a sense of being surrounded by invisible enemies? Did Regina feel it too?*

At the top of the stairs, they turned the other direction from the servants' bedrooms and attic. This part of the hallway was no better than the other. It was equally dark, dank, and grim.

"The children were kept in this part of the house?" Faith couldn't imagine such an arrangement. Nowadays, children were front and center in family life, with lovely rooms and tons of toys to prove it.

"It's like something out of a Victorian novel," Brooke said. "They probably ate gruel every day too."

At the end of the hallway, a door was open a crack. Chipped blue paint and a faded sign reading *Nursery* indicated they had found their destination.

Brooke pushed the door open all the way, and it swung back with a squeak of hinges.

The room was long and narrow, with slanted ceilings and dormer windows. The unpainted boards were worn, decorated here and there with scattered rag rugs. A line of metal beds, a crib, bookcases, bureaus, a ratty upholstered rocking chair, and a table and chairs furnished the room. Peeling, faded wallpaper depicting trains and dolls provided the only note of bygone cheer besides the vintage toys on the shelves.

Watson entered the room and sniffed at a teddy bear, a stray block, and around the table and chairs.

"Good luck finding scraps of food," Faith teased. "They'd be petrified by now."

Watson dived under the closest bed.

"When do you think this room was last used?" Brooke asked. She wandered over to a bookcase and motioned to a row of five baby dolls. "This looks like a set of those Dionne Quintuplet dolls. I saw a set like this on a show about antique toys."

Faith joined her at the bookcase and examined the dolls. "I think they were born in the 1930s, so they're from Violet's era." She glanced around the nursery, which was forlorn without young occupants playing and talking. Even crying would be better than this dusty silence.

"Look at this." Brooke hunkered down, reaching between the two bottom shelves. "There's a crack in the wall behind the bookcase."

Faith knelt, moving aside a train set and wooden pull toys. "There's a door back there. By the size of it, I'd guess it's one of those under-eave storage closets."

The bookcase easily pulled away, and Brooke unlatched the door. Inside the closet were several trunks, a few cardboard boxes, and a small plaid suitcase.

"Shall we?" Brooke's smile was wide. "Maybe the porcelain statue is in here after all."

One trunk held antique baby clothes for both girls and boys, including christening gowns, rompers, bonnets, and dresses. Another contained sheets and blankets. The boxes were full of books and toys even older than what was displayed. Most were battered and ripped but too well loved and precious to throw away.

They were halfway through the boxes when Faith realized she

hadn't seen her cat for a while. "I wonder where Watson is." She uncoiled from her seat on the floor. "I'd better find out what he's up to."

With a cry of frustration, the cat batted at the alluring piece of paper. He didn't like it when playthings didn't cooperate. This one was wedged in a crack between the floorboards, sticking out far enough that he knew it wanted to be rescued.

Aha! The paper edged out slightly, far enough for him to see it was one of those things called a photograph. His owner would like this as a gift. She spent hours and hours looking at photographs, even ones that didn't feature him.

He still couldn't quite grasp it. This was going to require both paws—and claws. He took a deep breath and pounced. Claws out. Engagement made. Now pull. Gently, gently . . .

Faith pulled the bed out, hoping Watson didn't have a mouse cornered.

He sat innocently between the bed and baseboard, one paw on a scrap of paper, staring up at her proudly.

Faith reached down and slid the paper out from under his paw. It was an old photograph. A group of men and women posed on what Faith recognized as Wintersea's terrace. The women wore dark dresses and aprons, the men work clothes or jackets and ties. Servants' attire.

Brooke peered over Faith's shoulder. "Who are they?"

Faith flipped the photo over. Names were penciled on the back in the order people were posed. "Rosie Whitcomb, Gertrude Lloyd, Maisie Wilkes, Benjamin Baker, Harold Gates, Ralph Briggs, and Carl Danbury."

"Danbury? Do you think he's related to the housekeeper?"

"Maybe." Faith turned the picture over again and studied the faces. Rosie was blonde and pert, Gertrude was dark-haired with a beaked nose, and Maisie was plump and smiling.

The men were also a mixed bag. Good-looking but aloof, Carl and Benjamin wore ties indicating their status as house servants. Ralph was burly and handsome, standing with arms crossed, smirking, and Harold was lean, wiry, and unsmiling. He leaned on a pitchfork, as if his rubber boots and overalls weren't enough to identify his occupation.

"Ralph Briggs is the man the police thought strangled Violet," Brooke reminded her.

"Too bad Regina didn't say in her manuscript who she thought was involved with Ralph. Maybe it was one of these people." Faith waved the photo. "Since Ralph is in this picture, we know it was taken before the murder. Let's scan it and send it to Eileen. She can research these names for us."

Brooke regarded Watson, who was washing nearby. "He deserves an extra treat for finding that photograph."

"That's my boy." Faith bent to stroke his head. "Always coming through for me. He's the best."

He blinked at her as if to say, "I know."

They continued searching the trunks and boxes but found nothing else related to the mystery, so they shoved everything back into the closet.

"I guess Regina wasn't lying when she said she moved the figurine and the letters," Brooke said. "I was hoping it was a bluff, in case someone read her manuscript."

Faith started to wipe her hands on her pants, then eyed her

dusty palms ruefully. She slapped them together a few times instead. "Why didn't she leave them in here? No one comes in this room anymore, judging by the amount of dust and dirt."

Brooke rose, using Faith's shoulder as a crutch. "She must have wanted them close at hand, a place where only she would go."

Their eyes met, and Faith knew by Brooke's expression that she shared her conclusion. "Her bedroom."

Gravel crunched outside, and Brooke went to look out the window. "The TV truck is here. I guess we'll have to wait to see if Ava wants to search Regina's bedroom."

"That's for certain. Ava's going to be consumed by the interview for the next few hours. We shouldn't distract her with this," Faith said. "Let's go clean up. She'll be looking for me."

The small television crew was setting up equipment in the parlor—a camera, microphones, and recording equipment. Mrs. Danbury kept an eagle eye on their progress. Roger and Sean loitered nearby, watching the proceedings.

Brooke and Watson joined them, but Faith spared the activity only a glance. Through the open door, she glimpsed the newswoman— identified by her skirt suit, big hair, and heavy makeup—bend to pet the cat. *Watson, always a ham!*

In her room, she hid the photograph in a dictionary, then washed her hands and face and changed into a skirt and a nicer sweater. She brushed her hair and put on a touch of lipstick. She wasn't going to be on camera, thank goodness, but she wanted to look professional for her role as Ava's librarian.

Noting with dismay that her quick primping session had taken longer than she'd intended and it was now after the time the interview was supposed to start, Faith rushed downstairs to see how things were going. She saw an impatient newswoman tapping her foot, bored sound and cameramen playing on their phones, and worried glances between the other guests at Wintersea. She didn't see Ava.

She approached Sean and whispered, "Hey, where's Ava?"

"That's what we're all wondering. The crew is talking about packing up and leaving," he whispered back.

That's odd. "Let me see if I can find her. She's probably just taking longer to get ready than she thought." Faith raced up the stairs and buzzed down the hall to Ava's room.

Instead of the excited greeting she expected when she knocked, she heard nothing.

A door opened down the hall, and Cassandra emerged from her room.

Faith called, "Have you seen Ava?"

The professor headed toward her. "Not since lunch. She said she was going to be up here getting ready." The redhead checked her watch. "Shouldn't she be downstairs giving her interview? It was supposed to start fifteen minutes ago."

Faith knocked again. "No one knows where she is. We can't let her miss the interview." On impulse, she tested the doorknob. It was unlocked. But Faith hesitated.

"Go ahead and check on her. Maybe she's napping." Cassandra glanced toward the stairs.

Taking a deep breath and praying she wasn't making a mistake, Faith opened the door. The bedroom was dim, curtains drawn against the day. "Ava?" she called.

Again, no answer.

She turned to Cassandra. "I don't see her."

Cassandra pushed past her. "She's sleeping. See?"

A long shape lay swaddled in the big bed. Faith squinted, making out the tangle of Ava's curly hair sticking out from the covers.

Cassandra hurried into the room and perched on the bed. "Ava? Ava, honey, the television crew is here. Everyone's waiting on you." She shook Ava's shoulder. Then again, firmly this time. She turned to Faith, her expression full of fear. "She's not waking up."

Her heart pounding, Faith ran to the bedside. She switched on a lamp, then bent to examine Ava. Her complexion was pale, her pulse light but steady under Faith's fingertips, and she was breathing regularly. But nothing they did roused her.

Winslow barged into the room. "My wife needs to be downstairs. The television crew is nearly out of patience."

"She's not going anywhere," Cassandra said. "She's out like a light."

Ava's husband moved to the bedside. He reached down and gently shook her shoulder. "Ava? Time to wake up, sweetheart." When she didn't respond, he sighed. "She gets like this sometimes. With her insomnia and sleepwalking, she really conks out when she does fall asleep."

"What a time to take a nap." Cassandra moved toward the door. "I'll tell the station that the interview is canceled."

"Be careful what you say." Winslow's tone was sharp. "Don't embarrass her."

Cassandra drew herself up. "You know me better than that. I'll say Ava is ill, that's all."

Despite Winslow's explanation, Faith sensed there was something wrong about Ava's slumber. It was too deep. "I think we should try to wake her up. Just in case something is wrong."

Winslow sent her a look. "What do you mean?" But he sat on the bed and started to prod and shake Ava in earnest.

Faith noticed a cup of tea beside the bed, and out of curiosity, she picked it up and sniffed it. Herbal. *Did she have a reaction maybe?*

Ava stirred with a moan. Her eyelashes fluttered, and a moment later she pushed herself to a seated position. "What are you two doing here?" Alarm flashed over her face. "The television interview. I can't miss that."

Winslow put a staying hand on her arm. "It's over, Ava. You slept through it." He had to restrain her with hands on her shoulders. "Everything will be all right. We'll reschedule. In the meantime, I'm taking you away for a couple of days. You need to rest before the conference starts."

Faith began to slip from the room, wanting to give them privacy.

Winslow's voice stopped her. "Faith, please find out if the other professors can check in at Castleton early. I'd like to close the house while we're gone."

Faith's belly clenched. She hoped Castleton Manor was ready for guests—and that Marlene was too. "I'll call Marlene and have her get in touch with you." The final arrangements would have to be hammered out between Winslow and the assistant manager.

It looks like Ava is all right, thank goodness. Faith pushed away her lingering uneasiness about the situation. It was time to retrieve all of Castleton's books, pack up, and go home.

When Faith parked in front of the gardener's cottage a couple of hours later, she was surprised to find tears of relief in her eyes. Being at Wintersea had been more of an ordeal than she realized.

With a little laugh, she blinked the tears away. "I'm getting foolish in my old age," she told Watson, who sat next to her in the passenger seat. "But it feels wonderful to be home."

After gathering as much as she could carry, Faith unlocked the door using her juggling skills and pushed it open with her knee. Watson raced inside. The house was chilly, so after setting everything down, she turned up the heat and started a fire. Unpacking could wait.

She hadn't eaten dinner, so the next order of business was searching through her freezer for something to eat. Fortunately she'd frozen leftovers before leaving for Wintersea. She found a tub of Eileen's lasagna and put it in the microwave to thaw. She filled Watson's dishes, to his delight, and put on the kettle for tea.

Faith remembered that she needed to scan the photograph of Wintersea's servants and e-mail it to Eileen. She prepared a cup of tea and carried it to her desk, where she set up her laptop. In a few minutes she sent her aunt a clear image that included Watson's claw marks in the corner.

By then the lasagna was ready for the cook setting and Watson was demanding a treat. She foraged and found one last tunaroon from Midge's pet bakery. She held it up for him to see. "This will have to do until I can get downtown again."

Seeming to take her seriously, the cat snatched the treat and carried it to the fireside, where he plopped down and licked it, holding it between his front paws. He usually gobbled up his favorite treats, but he seemed intent on savoring this one.

Someone knocked on the front door.

Not for the first time, Faith wished there was a peephole in the door. But she had a sneaking suspicion who had come calling. Perhaps it was the aura of doom that had descended.

She was right.

Marlene Russell stood on the step, dressed in a long wool coat, shoulders hunched against the cold. "Well, don't just stand there staring at me. Let me in. I'm freezing."

"Come on in." The microwave dinged in the kitchen, and Faith imagined her meal inside, bubbling and hot. That was obviously going to have to wait. Faith reached for Marlene's coat.

But Marlene hugged her arms close. "I'm not staying long."

Thank heaven for small mercies. "Come stand by the fire at least." Without waiting for an answer, Faith led the way into her cozy living room. The fire needed another log, so she added one. "How are things?"

Marlene's upper lip curled. "About as good as one might expect, after having four demanding guests check in early."

"Four?" Faith counted Roger, Sean, and Cassandra. "Oh, did Stephanie come too?"

Marlene crossed her arms. "Oh yes. And she's a royal—" She stopped and swallowed the word she'd been about to say. "Nothing is right in her eyes. She's had the maids hopping, and she's barely arrived."

"I'm not surprised. They're pretty spoiled after having Mrs.

Danbury at their beck and call. Not to mention Brooke, who did an awesome job by the way." Might as well put in a plug for her friend.

An odd expression passed over Marlene's face. "Mrs. Danbury?"

"She's the housekeeper at Wintersea," Faith said as if she hadn't noticed Marlene's reaction. She kept talking, hoping to get more information. "Florabelle Danbury. Someone less likely to be named Florabelle I've never met."

Marlene made a dismissive gesture. "People can't help the foolishness of their parents. Back to the conference. I'd like you to work in the library tomorrow. Those professors had the nerve to ask *me* to find books for them." She sniffed. "Oh, and I do hope you're keeping track of the ones they have. Mr. Jaxon won't be pleased if some go missing."

Faith thought of the tote resting by her front door, full of Castleton volumes. She'd been planning to check them in the next morning. Hoping Marlene couldn't read her mind, she said, "I'll be over right after breakfast."

Marlene smiled. "Thank you."

Shocked by the assistant manager's uncharacteristic response, Faith stood there, speechless.

"I know this is extra work for you," Marlene added.

Faith started to worry that she was openly gaping.

Then Marlene became Marlene again. "But all of us at Castleton must go above and beyond." She marched toward the door. "Don't bother to show me out."

As soon as the door clicked shut behind her boss, Faith raced to the kitchen to reheat the lasagna. She also made a fresh cup of tea. Then she carried her dinner to her favorite armchair and prepared to dig in.

She'd enjoyed only one cheesy bite when someone rapped on the door.

Marlene again? If it was, she was going to keep eating, even if it was rude.

Wolfe stood on the steps, dressed in a navy wool overcoat, a jaunty cap on his head. "I hope I'm not bothering you."

What could she say? "Not at all. Please come in." Despite her best efforts, she couldn't restrain a glance over her shoulder at her plate.

"You're in the middle of eating. I'll come back."

Faith moved aside. "No, it's all right. Really."

Wolfe entered the foyer. "Only if you keep eating." He took off his gloves, tucked them into his pockets, then pulled off the cap and hung it along with his coat on a peg. He wore a fine suit, his usual business attire.

"Would you like some lasagna? A cup of tea? I have the imported brand you like." Faith's face flushed at the admission. On the way home, she'd stopped at McGinty's, and the pub had agreed to sell her a box. She'd told herself firmly that it was just because she had liked it so much, and it was only a bonus that Wolfe liked it too.

Wolfe rubbed his hands together. "I'd love some tea, but I won't steal your lasagna. I ate already."

"I'll only be a minute. Go ahead and warm up." As Faith headed for the kitchen, she saw him make a beeline for the crackling fire.

Watson lifted his head to study the intruder before sinking back into slumber.

The kettle was still hot, so the water boiled quickly. Faith made a pot of tea rather than a cup, knowing Wolfe preferred that. A pitcher of milk, a spoon, and a cup completed the tray.

He turned when she entered the room. "How nice. Thank you. Now eat your dinner, and I'll fix my own cup." He sat in an adjacent armchair and proceeded to pour.

Faith curled up in her chair and devoured a few bites while he was busy. "Anything new concerning your . . . problem?"

Wolfe patted the breast pocket of his suit jacket. "I'm afraid so. I got a ransom demand today." He reached to pull it out.

Faith made a startled objection. "Sorry. I was thinking you shouldn't handle it too much because of fingerprints."

"I already thought of that." The piece of paper he withdrew was sealed in a plastic bag. "And I had a feeling something was fishy about the envelope, so I used gloves to open it."

"Good thinking." Faith abandoned her fork and came over to Wolfe's chair.

He set the bag on a table and smoothed it out so she could read the note inside.

> *It's time to pay up. Put $100,000 in small, unmarked bills in a blue duffel bag and leave it by the Peter Pan fountain near your maze at midnight Friday. That's a down payment. No police! A social media campaign aimed at destroying you is ready to go. Expect a call confirming at nine o'clock tonight.*

"Wow," Faith said. "They actually did it. Are you going to pay them? What if they keep making demands?"

Wolfe's smile was sly. "They won't do this again. I'm going to set a trap."

"Really? How?" Faith sank back onto her chair. Her pasta was waiting, but she didn't feel like eating anymore.

"One of my investments is in a company that makes experimental electronic devices. I'm going to use a night-vision camera and film whoever it is when they come to pick up the money."

"Why not have them arrested right then?"

"I would if I could count on the discretion of my staff. In a place like Castleton, the word would be out in five minutes that the police were on-site. There's no way the blackmailer wouldn't find out."

Faith saw his point.

"I'll have someone stationed in the parking lot to see which car they get into. Then I'll call it in." Wolfe set his jaw. "Whoever it is has to be prosecuted, but I hope they're offered a lighter sentence so they reveal any accomplices."

Faith thought of Gwen Harrison. Were her husband and father-in-law involved? Was she? That reminded her of the incident with the stalker. "I had an unpleasant experience last night." As she relayed the story, Wolfe grew gratifyingly indignant.

"If it turns out that man scared you because of me, then forget what I said about a lighter sentence. I hope they throw the book at him." His brow creased in concern. "I'm sorry I got you involved."

"It's all right. I wanted to help." Faith had to admit she enjoyed the feeling of being cared about. Her ex-boyfriend wouldn't have noticed if she'd been mugged and bleeding. His main concern would have been whether or not she'd picked up his shirts at the dry cleaner. She smiled ruefully.

Wolfe raised his eyebrows.

"Sorry. Just a random thought."

He topped off his cup from the teapot. Cradling the hot beverage, he leaned back in his chair, stretching out his long legs toward the fire. "This is really nice. I've always thought this was such a cozy room."

"I love it. Living in this cottage is one of the best perks of my job."

Wolfe angled his head. "Better than taking orders from me?" His smile revealed he was joking.

Is he flirting? Faith kept her gaze on the flickering flames. "You're a great boss, and working at Castleton is a dream come true."

"You mean when it's not a nightmare." He laughed and she joined in.

They sat in companionable silence for a few minutes. Then Faith remembered that she had a container of ice cream in the freezer and some of Brooke's cookies. "Would you like dessert? I have cookies and ice cream, and I'm thinking they should be combined."

He eagerly agreed.

By the time they finished every sweet bite of Faith's cookie and ice cream sandwiches, the mantel clock was striking nine. As it finished, Wolfe's cell phone went off.

A thrill of dread flashed through Faith. "Is that the—?"

He nodded and put a finger to his lips. He activated the speakerphone function and set the phone on the table between their chairs. "Hello?"

A deep mechanized voice, reminiscent of horror movies, answered. "Is this Wolfe Jaxon?"

"It is. I assume this is the blackmailer?"

"Did you get my note?"

"I did."

Wolfe's clipped, short answer seemed to disconcert the caller, who went quiet.

"Hello? Are you there?" Wolfe asked, annoyed.

"Put the duffel at the fountain by midnight tomorrow night. Friday. No police, no witnesses, or I'll push the button. And you know what that means." There was a click, and the caller was gone.

Wolfe snatched up the phone to examine it, then slapped it down with a growl.

"Does that fake voice give you any clue who's doing this?" Faith asked.

"No. Anyone can download voice alteration software now." He picked up his phone and did a search. "See how many there are?" He displayed the screen to Faith.

She was impressed by the array. "The fact that they changed their voice proves something. You must know this person, or why would they bother disguising their voice?"

"That's a good thought. Whoever it is might just be covering his or her tracks, but I think it's more likely someone who was on that boat, like we've been surmising all along." Wolfe scrolled through his phone. "I learned that my former captain is back in town." He handed her the phone.

In the photo a burly man in his late thirties stood proudly at the wheel of a yacht. The caption read, *Enjoying my new gig as captain of* Sophie May, *berthed in Lighthouse Bay. See you sailors next summer!* The man's wide grin was attractive, but his remarkably thick eyebrows and heavy beard caught Faith's attention.

"I've seen this man. He was at The Swooping Seagull when I visited."

"Is that so?" Wolfe rubbed his chin. "As they say in bad novels, the plot thickens."

19

The next day, Friday, the atmosphere at Castleton Manor had the urgency of a held breath. No matter what Faith did or where she went, in the back of her mind lingered the knowledge that the blackmailer would strike at midnight. On top of that worry was the stress of the conference, due to begin the next day.

Preparations for the event were gearing up. The full staff arrived on-site. Food was delivered. The gallery was set up with chairs and a podium for the opening keynote. Faith helped with last-minute tasks—making sure packets were copied and ready, the attendee list was complete, and that all the speakers were going to show up.

This last issue was especially problematic due to the inclement weather. The rain had intensified, and strong thunderstorms were forecast for the entire weekend. Travel was expected to become treacherous, and some flights had already been canceled.

As for the planning trio, tempers were short. "I told you we should have had it in June," Cassandra snarled.

"No one wants to go to these things in the summer," Roger snarled back. "They want to be outside in their little gardens."

"Don't worry about it, you two," Sean said. "In a few months no one will even remember what did or didn't happen." The Irishman seemed subdued, almost depressed.

Finally they went off to their rooms to get ready for dinner and left Faith alone in the library. She spent the early evening performing the almost mindless task of shelving books, savoring the peace of her sanctuary. Watson was sleeping on a chair near the fire, and the room was dead quiet. *The lull before the storm.* Starting tomorrow, the manor would be bustling with guests. The library was always a focus of activity, and Faith often worked odd hours during retreats.

Not that she minded. She loved her job. But she also adored being alone with the vast treasury of books that was the Castleton Manor library.

A rap on the half-open door startled her. She turned her head carefully, mindful of her precarious position high on the rolling ladder. With a leap of her pulse, she saw Wolfe in the doorway, the flickering fire casting light and shadow across his tall figure. Faith had left the room dim, with only a few lamps and sconces turned on to chase away the gloom.

"There you are." Wolfe laughed. "I didn't see you on your perch."

Faith slid a book into its spot, then climbed down. She waited to speak until she had almost reached his side. "Would you like to sit?" She gestured at the long velvet seat in front of the fire.

"We seem to make a habit of sitting by warm fires, don't we?" Wolfe said lightly. He glanced toward the French doors, where rain dashed against the panes. "Although on a night like this, there's no better place."

"Are you all set for—you know?" Faith asked.

"I am. The equipment is in and working. Now we wait for midnight."

The clock on the mantel behind them chimed the hour, the sound loud in the hush, and they jumped, then laughed nervously.

"Talk about perfect timing," Wolfe said.

"Can I stand watch with you?" Faith asked, surprising herself. "I'd like to see this to its conclusion."

Wolfe studied her face. "I don't see why not. I got you involved, after all. And we'll be safe inside."

"Take me through the plan."

Several hours later, Faith was in the library again, but now the door was locked and she and Wolfe were watching a computer monitor that displayed a view of the Peter Pan fountain, one of the garden features near the maze. The blue duffel bag was on the lip of the bowl. All the lights in the room were out so they could see the driveway through the windows. It was a distance away, but at night, headlights were clearly visible.

Wolfe's phone rang, and again he put it on speakerphone. "Hello, Chief Garris. How are you?"

"The weather stinks, but other than that we're fine," Lighthouse Bay's chief of police said. "We're waiting in unmarked cars as you requested. You sure you don't want us to come onto the property?"

"Absolutely not. One whiff of you guys and this bird will be in the wind. I've got the camera going. After the target picks up the duffel, I'll call you. I've got someone in the parking lot monitoring cars, so we'll have the make and model."

They heard murmuring on the other end of the line. Then Chief Garris said, "Wolfe, let's keep a live connection from 11:58 on. Give me the blow-by-blow account, okay?"

They agreed and ended the call.

Faith and Wolfe settled in to wait. The view of the fountain remained static, only the heavy rain and the wind gusting through the trees revealing that it was a video, not a still photograph.

Faith stared so intently that she had to blink to clear her vision when she spied a shape moving in the corner of the screen. She blinked again, then squinted. "Look. Someone is coming."

Garris called and asked for an update.

"The blackmailer is approaching," Wolfe announced. "He isn't making very good progress. He seems to be keeping low to the ground and weaving in and out of the trees, probably to make sure we don't see him."

Faith pulled on her coat and slid her feet into boots. She dropped her cell phone into her coat pocket.

He muted his phone. "What are you doing?"

"I'm going outside." Faith tugged a hat over her head and winked. "To search for my cat."

Wolfe glanced at Watson, sitting on the velvet settee, and comprehension dawned on his face. He rose from his chair. "I'm going with you."

"But won't seeing you scare the blackmailer away? He's trying to keep his identity hidden from you."

Wolfe grabbed his coat. "I know all the shortcuts. We'll see him, but he won't see us." He pressed his lips together. "I can't allow you to be out there alone in case anything goes wrong."

Faith didn't argue. He was right.

Wolfe finished putting on his outerwear, then checked the camera again. "He's almost reached the fountain," he told Garris.

Once they left the shelter of the building, wind laced with rain scoured Faith's face. She ducked her head and plodded across the sodden ground behind Wolfe. He cut across the grass, a route that Faith knew led directly to the fountain.

As Faith moved through the storm, her mind's eye roamed ahead to her destination.

Wolfe went to the right and into a copse of trees. Faith darted between two trunks and almost tripped over him. He lay flat on the ground, groaning softly.

Fear lanced Faith. Had he been attacked? "Wolfe, what's wrong?"

"I tripped and fell." He pushed himself to a sitting position and felt his ankle. "I might have sprained it. It certainly hurts enough." He reached out a hand. "Please help me up."

It quickly became apparent that Wolfe couldn't move faster than a crawl since he couldn't put much weight on the injured foot.

"Faith, I hate to say it, but you'll have to go the rest of the way by yourself. Stay out of sight, okay?"

Faith's core tightened in determination. It was up to her now. "Of course." At his direction, she traversed the rest of the small forest, her goal the cedar hedge surrounding the fountain.

The blackmailer would pass right by her hiding place as he headed to the parking lot. A number of lamps illuminated this part of the garden, orbs of gold in the dark. Faith could follow, unseen, and at some point she would be able to see his face.

Faith reached the massive hedge, halting in a gap that gave her a view of the fountain. A light burned there too, bright enough to reveal someone approaching the duffel bag. The figure was short, much smaller than she expected. *They must have sent Gwen.*

The person seized the bag and trudged away. Her route would take her right past where Faith was hiding. But instead of turning in the direction of the parking lot, the person tramped directly toward her.

Alarmed, Faith jumped backward, becoming tangled in the dense branches. Her coat caught on a branch, and she fought to get it untangled. *Get away! Escape!*

"What are you doing out here?"

Heart leaping into her throat, Faith turned to see Cassandra staring at her. *Cassandra? She's the blackmailer? Why is she blackmailing Wolfe?*

Faith thrust her confusion aside. "I'm looking for my cat. I let him out a while ago, and he didn't come back." She finally wrenched her coat away from the clutching branches. "I thought I heard him meowing over here."

"I hope you find him. I've got to get going." Lugging her burden, the professor waddled away toward the mansion.

Faith let her move a distance away, then pulled out her cell phone and texted Wolfe. *Cassandra Cooper has the duffel. She's coming your way.* Keeping her gaze on the small figure, Faith went in the same direction.

Cassandra veered off toward the parking lot.

Faith hesitated. Should she update Wolfe? *No time.* Cassandra was going to leave with the money, probably to hide it somewhere, and then it would be Faith's word against hers.

Slipping on the wet pavement and splashing through puddles, Faith stumbled toward the parked cars. For a flash, she had a vision of how the slow-motion pursuit must look from a bird's-eye view—two women struggling in the rain. She prayed that Wolfe would tell the police to drive onto the property.

She caught up to Cassandra in the parking lot. "Where are you going?"

Cassandra was unlocking an older model sedan with a key and didn't even turn to look. "What's it to you?" She opened the driver's side door and hefted the duffel in.

Faith pounced, shoving the heavy door against Cassandra's leg, trapping her half-in, half-out of the car. "I can't let you leave. Not until you give Wolfe his money back."

"What are you talking about? Those are my gym clothes." She pushed the door back against Faith. "Let me go."

With a grunt, Faith braced her boots on the pavement. "Throw your keys on the ground and I will."

"You're crazy."

"Why'd you do it, Cassandra? You've got a good life. Teaching job, book deal—"

"And tons of debt. You know how much it costs to get your doctorate? Oh, that's right, *you* probably wouldn't. What do you have? A master's?"

Faith ignored this slur on her educational attainment, resisting the rejoinder that at least she knew enough to avoid committing crimes.

As if reading her mind, Cassandra said, "If you don't let me go, I'll have you arrested for unlawful detainment. How's that gonna look, smarty-pants?"

"I don't understand. How did you know what happened on Wolfe's yacht?"

Cassandra hooted with laughter tinged with hysteria. "Wolfe's *yacht*," she mocked. "I was the cook. That was my summer job, making food for snotty rich girls. Of course they didn't eat much. No sugar, no fat, no carbs. Oh, how I wanted to scream at them to shut up!"

To Faith's intense relief, she spotted headlights coming over the rise. *Took them long enough.* To distract Cassandra, she said, "I can see how that would annoy you. We have many finicky guests here too."

"They weren't finicky—they were spoiled rotten. Kept me on the run day and night. Especially that Valentina chick. She was the worst. At least she got what she deserved. And now I've got what I deserve—money and a new life waiting for me."

The dots connected in Faith's head. Shock made her loosen her stance against the car door.

With a cry of triumph, Cassandra rammed the door and sent Faith flying. Then in one deft motion, she yanked it shut and started the car. She fishtailed out of the space and tore across the lot.

Instinctively, Faith ran after the car but soon realized how foolish that was. She stopped and bent down, gulping in air.

A tall, limping figure appeared. Wolfe. "Faith, are you all right?"

"I'm fine." She straightened. "But Cassandra killed your fiancée."

20

Wolfe staggered, resting a hand on Faith's shoulder for support. "What are you saying?"

Down the hill, blue lights flashed. The police were announcing their presence.

"Cassandra Cooper was a cook on your yacht. I think she had something to do with Valentina's death." Faith looked toward the flashing lights, just as the sound of a heavy thump reached them. "I hope the police managed to stop her. Let's go see."

They slowly made their way down the drive, Faith assisting Wolfe as he hobbled along.

Cassandra's car rested against a huge pine, the hood crumpled. Chief Garris was cuffing the woman's hands.

Cassandra twisted and snarled. "Why are you arresting me? I'm going to sue you for making me crash." Then she spotted Wolfe. "I'll take you for everything you're worth. Your resort isn't safe for guests. You'll end up as poor as me."

Officer Laddy opened the passenger door and pulled out the blue duffel bag.

Now Wolfe spoke. "You'll find $100,000 in marked twenties in there, as we planned."

"Marked?" Cassandra screamed. "I specifically told you unmarked. You evil, horrible—" The rest of her vitriol was lost as Chief Garris ducked her head and put her in the back seat of his cruiser.

"She came racing down the hill," Laddy said. "When she saw us waiting, she lost control and smashed into that tree."

Chief Garris joined them. "Fortunately no one was hurt." His lips quirked. "I have a feeling you weren't expecting the blackmailer to be one of your guests."

"It seems we crossed paths before," Wolfe said. "Although I never met her. I left hiring of the crew to my captain. After Valentina died, I didn't take that boat out again. I sold it."

"She was a cook on Wolfe's boat," Faith filled in. "I think she had something to do with Valentina going overboard." She relayed what Cassandra had said word for word. "Of course you can't use that, right?"

"No, it's hearsay. But we can question her," Garris said. "I'll get a wrecker over here to move the car. Then we'll be out of your way."

The Great Hall Gallery rang with the sound of excited voices as guests mingled, enjoying delicious appetizers and beverages. The opening reception of the Gothic Studies conference was under way and, despite the continuing stormy weather, the attendance was as expected.

Dressed in a gold chiffon skirt and a sequined black sweater, Faith stood watching from the sidelines.

Marlene clicked up to her on high heels. "Did they get another keynote?" She frowned at her wristwatch. "We're due to begin in fifteen minutes."

"Ava is going to do it," Faith said.

After Cassandra had been arrested, the conference committee had an emergency early-morning meeting, connecting to the Winterbournes via phone. Ava Winterbourne was tapped to do the speech at her husband's insistence. Since he was sponsoring the event, there wasn't much argument from Roger or Sean.

Rested and happy, Ava and Winslow had arrived that afternoon and checked into the Jane Austen Suite, where a hundred pink roses and two bottles of rare champagne waited for them.

A Castleton employee scurried into the room carrying a stand and set it near the entrance. On it was a hastily printed poster of Ava with the headline *Gothic in Real Life: Ava Winterbourne*. Ava was going ahead with the Regina Winterbourne project, despite objections from the other professors. Even Cassandra wrote a scathing letter from jail to Ava, calling her a limelight hog.

"I don't care who does it," Marlene snapped. "As long as we stay on schedule so dinner is served on time. They've made the agenda far too tight." She glared at Faith as though it was her fault.

"I'm sure everything will be fine," Faith said. Whether it was or not was certainly not in her control, but it didn't pay to argue with Marlene.

"You'd better hope so." With a toss of her head, Marlene stormed off.

"What's she upset about?" Wolfe appeared at her side.

Faith tried to hide how surprised she was to see him. Ever since Cassandra had confessed to pushing Valentina off his yacht, Wolfe had been holed up in his apartment. Faith didn't blame him. It must have felt like losing his fiancée all over again.

"It's the first night of a conference. She's always like that, remember?" Faith took in his elegant black suit, white dress shirt, and tie with miniscule skulls and crossbones on a black background. "Nice tie, by the way."

"Thanks. I thought it was appropriate for the conference." Watching the crowd, Wolfe absently smoothed it into place. "Good turnout despite the storm."

"I'm sure they think it adds to the atmosphere. Can't have a Gothic conference in sunny weather."

"I wish I'd been aware of that when we scheduled." His tone was ironic.

Faith glanced at a nearby clock. "I'd better go find Ava. It's almost time for the keynote."

"See you at dinner, perhaps?" He waited for her agreement before disappearing into the throng.

Faith made a circuit of the room looking for Ava, but she wasn't chatting, eating, or sitting near the podium. She didn't see Roger or

Winslow, but Sean was standing near the statue of Agatha Christie, listening to two garrulous women. By the way he tilted his head and clasped his hands behind his back, she could tell he was patiently humoring them.

Sean spotted Faith, and relief washed over his features. "Excuse me, ladies."

They released him with twitters and giggles.

"Have you seen Ava?" Faith asked him.

"No, not since she and Winslow arrived. She promised to join me down here for a preconference chat, but she hasn't shown up."

Faith scanned the room. Attendees were taking seats in anticipation of the presentation. "I'd better go upstairs and fetch her. Maybe she lost track of time."

"I'll come with you," Sean said, his brow creased with worry. "I hope she's okay."

"She seemed fine earlier." Faith weaved through the people standing in the open archway to the main hall. "Is there something in particular you're worried about?"

"After that last episode at Wintersea I started wondering if Ava suffers from the fear of success." Sean paused to let a cluster of guests pass.

Faith was puzzled. "I've heard of fear of failure."

"Both have the same effect. They keep people stuck," Sean said as they climbed the staircase, a marble edifice that curved up to the second story, where wrought iron balconies overlooked the area. "People who suffer from the fear of success syndrome choke when they almost reach their goals. Flunk a test, miss an important presentation, don't complete—"

"Their dissertation," Faith finished for him. She had to raise her voice to be heard in the vast space, which was filled with echoes as people ascended and descended the stairs, greeting friends with cries of excitement.

Faith knocked on the door of the Jane Austen Suite.

Winslow answered, a half-knotted tie around his neck. "How are you two tonight?" He released the knob and continued to knot the tie.

"We're fine. Thanks," Faith said. "Is Ava here? It's almost time for her speech."

Winslow frowned. "Ava went downstairs half an hour ago. She said something about meeting with you, Sean, and Roger."

"She never showed up," Sean said, "and I haven't seen Roger since before the reception."

"Stephanie's among the missing too," Winslow said. "She was supposed to take dictation for me this afternoon, but she never did."

Faith's phone rang in her bag, playing the tune she used to identify calls from Eileen. "Let me take this." She stepped away a few paces. "Hi, Aunt Eileen. We've got a bit of a crisis here."

"I won't keep you long. But I thought you'd like to know I found a connection between one of the servants in that picture you sent and one of your professors—Roger Lewis. Gertrude Lloyd was his grandmother."

Faith thought back to the photograph of the servants. Now that she knew of the relationship, she could see a resemblance. Both Roger and Gertrude were dark, with beaked noses and a stern demeanor. "Did you find out anything else?"

"I sure did." Eileen's voice rose in pitch. "Gertrude was questioned when Violet died. According to a source I found, there was a rumor that Gertrude and the assailant, Ralph Briggs, were involved. Although the police apparently couldn't prove anything, she was deported to England soon after. I'm sure Violet's husband had something to do with that."

Regina must have learned all this too. And the knowledge might have killed her. "I can't thank you enough," Faith said hastily, "but I have to hang up now."

"Problem with the conference?" Her aunt's tone was sympathetic.

"You could say that. I'll call you later." Faith disconnected. Returning to the men, she said, "We need to go back to Wintersea. I think Ava's life is in danger."

Winslow dug in his pocket for his keys. "Let's go. I'm driving."

The trio paused only long enough to grab outerwear, then bolted out of the manor into the thunderstorm. Winslow's Volvo SUV was still parked near the portico, where the valet had left it earlier.

"Be careful," the valet called. "It's dangerous out there. You should have seen the guy who left half an hour ago. His little car was hydroplaning all over the place."

"That sounds like Roger," Sean said. "He's not that far ahead of us."

"Did he have two women with him?" Faith asked the valet.

The valet shrugged. "Just one. A lovely woman with curly dark hair."

"My wife," Winslow said grimly as they pulled away, splashing through large puddles. "And I pray to God that she's all right."

As they drove through the pouring rain, Faith filled them in from the back seat about Eileen's discoveries. "Regina must have made the connection with Roger too."

"Why would Roger do such a thing?" Winslow said.

"Academic jealousy," Sean said crisply. "Roger's grandmother was integral to the story. He probably feels the telling of it belongs to him and no one else."

Winslow slowed to make the corner through the gate at Wintersea. "Hang on. The road is almost flooded." He handed Sean his phone. "Call the police, will you? I don't know what we'll find."

As Sean dialed, Faith heard a familiar meow. At first she thought she was hearing things. She shook her head to clear it. No, there it was again. "Watson, are you in here?"

Her cat leaped over the seat from the rear compartment.

Despite her tension and fear, Faith laughed, gathering him in her arms.

Winslow stole a glance in the rearview mirror. "Stowaway?"

"He must have gotten in when we had the door open. I don't understand how the valet didn't see him."

Sean was on the phone to the police, explaining that they were needed at Wintersea to check out a possible crime in progress. When he hung up, he said, "They'll be here as soon as they can. Right now they're dealing with accidents on opposite sides of town."

"I guess it's up to us," Faith said. Her words were brave, but inwardly she quivered. *What if we're too late?*

They made it to the house without incident. A flash of lightning illuminated a tiny blue car and a black sedan parked in front.

"Stephanie and Roger are both here," Sean said.

"And they're not leaving until I say so." Winslow parked in a way that blocked the cars in. He turned off the engine and took the fob. "Let's roll." He ran up the steps and unlocked the front door.

Faith, Sean, and Watson hurried to keep up.

"Mrs. Danbury!" Winslow bellowed.

The housekeeper burst into the foyer. "Mr. Winterbourne, I didn't—I thought—"

"Enough." Winslow scanned the adjacent rooms. "Where is my wife?"

"Your wife?" Mrs. Danbury gawked at him. "She's . . . not with you?" This last word was a squeak. She wrapped her hands in her apron, twisting them.

"No, she's not with me." He advanced toward the housekeeper until he loomed over her. "She's here somewhere. With Roger and Stephanie."

Horror flashed over Mrs. Danbury's face. "Stephanie? Why, she's at the conference—" She burst into tears.

The two men stormed away, Sean thumping upstairs and Winslow searching the downstairs rooms. Watson trotted off.

Faith lingered. "You didn't know that your niece was involved?"

Mrs. Danbury used her apron to wipe her face. "I thought . . . I wanted to help."

Faith guessed where she was going. "Stephanie wants to be Winslow's wife, doesn't she? You thought you'd help by making things uncomfortable for Regina and Ava."

"I only wanted to chase them away, not—"

"Kill them," Faith finished for her. "Please give me the keys to the tower and the tunnel. That's where they are, right?"

Mrs. Danbury grabbed the keys hanging from her belt and pulled off two with shaking fingers. "They could be . . . I'm not sure."

Faith snatched the keys. Whether or not Mrs. Danbury was lying, they needed to get into the tower now. Otherwise Wintersea might experience yet another mysterious death. Then she thought of something. "Do you have a cell phone?"

The housekeeper shook her head, emptying her pockets to show she wasn't lying. Even so, she might have one somewhere else. Or she might use the landline to call Stephanie and warn her.

"Give me the rest of your keys," Faith ordered.

Mrs. Danbury hesitated.

"I can have Winslow ask you instead."

The woman unclipped the keys and handed them to Faith.

"I hate to do this, but I have to lock you in the pantry." Faith shooed the woman along to the kitchen. When the housekeeper was safely inside the enclosed, windowless space, Faith found the key and locked the door. "You'll be all right," she called. "At least you have food."

Faith turned and ran back through the house, shouting, "Winslow, Sean, to the tower!" Then she returned to the kitchen and foraged for a flashlight in the drawers.

There were two routes to the building, across the yard and through the tunnel. Due to the stormy conditions, Faith voted for the tunnel. Flashlight in hand and Watson right beside her, she was opening the cellar door when Winslow and Sean rushed in. To her shock, she noticed Winslow was carrying a shotgun.

"Are you going to use that?" Sean asked, pointing at the gun.

"I hope not," Winslow said. He patted his pocket and pulled out a pistol. "Here you go."

Sean took it gingerly and tucked it into his own pocket. "I hope I don't shoot my foot off."

"That would be quite a trick," Winslow said, "especially since the safety is on."

Down in the cellar, gloomy despite the lights, Faith remembered all too well the route to the tunnel. As she expected, the door was locked. She unlocked it, then stood back to let the men go ahead, Watson darting in front of them. She shone the light so they could see.

Sean groaned when he hit his head for the second time on the low ceiling. "Where are you leading us? This place is as dark and narrow as a mine shaft."

"This is an alternate route to the tower," Winslow called back. "Or would you prefer to get caught up in that storm outside?"

At the other end, the door was locked as well. The men waited while Faith used the second key, grateful that Mrs. Danbury had cooperated.

Once through the door, they hesitated, Winslow putting a finger to his lips. "Quiet. We need to surprise them." Tucking his gun more firmly under his arm, he crept up the staircase in a smooth, noiseless gait.

Sean and Faith followed him, and Watson dashed ahead and reached the top first.

The second-floor room was empty.

"Where are they?" Sean asked.

Winslow pointed to the ceiling, his eyes steely.

Faith took a deep breath as the implications sank in. Roger, Ava, and Stephanie were on the top floor of the tower, an open deck edged by battlements. Where Regina had jumped. Allegedly.

Moving swiftly, Winslow went to a door and opened it. A curving staircase led to the roof. He gestured for them to wait, then bounded lightly up the steep stairs, still holding the shotgun. Watson accompanied him.

"You'd think he was a college kid on a frolic," Sean whispered to Faith.

A moment later Winslow came back around the corner and motioned for them to come up.

Pulse pounding, chest tight with fear, Faith climbed the flight of stairs, hoping and praying they'd be able to rescue Ava without anyone getting hurt.

At the top, the layout was such that they could peer around a bulwark and see the open area while remaining hidden.

Faith's heart plummeted when she took in the scene. Stephanie and Roger flanked Ava, who was facing outward, toward the ocean. Each held one of her arms.

"You know you want to, love," Roger crooned. "Just step up. All your problems will be over."

Ava swayed in his grip. "No, I don't want . . ." Her words were slurred.

She must be drugged. Faith wanted to cry out, to run and rescue her, but she held herself in check. She sensed the same reaction in the men, especially Winslow, who practically seethed with suppressed rage.

Roger, with the intuition that seemed all too common in evil people, turned his head. "Whoever is there, one move and she's over the edge."

That was too much for Winslow. He stepped out into the open and lifted the shotgun to his shoulder. "Let her go. And I might let you live."

Roger sneered. "Bad move, sir." To Stephanie he said, "One, two . . ." They lifted Ava by the underarms.

"Stop. Don't do it." Winslow's voice broke as he lowered the gun. "What do you want?"

The British professor practically danced with glee. "Why, I want to be the one to write about my own grandmother and the murder of Violet Winterbourne. I've already got Hollywood producers lined up to buy the rights." He yanked Ava's arm. "All I need is the figurine and those letters. But she won't tell me where they are."

"She doesn't know," Faith said. "No one does. Only Regina did, and she's dead."

Roger glared at Stephanie. "If you hadn't been so hasty in pushing Regina, we'd be all set."

"*You'd* be all set, you mean," the secretary retorted. "I'd still have yet another bimbo wife to deal with."

While this exchange was going on, Watson had crept out from his hiding place. Staying in the shadows, he padded silently around the circumference of the platform.

Faith elbowed Sean covertly. He got the picture and passed along the information to Winslow with a tug on the back of his shirt. The two men subtly shifted their stance. They were ready.

Once Watson was a few feet from Roger, he stopped, looking over his shoulder at Faith. Then he leaped lightly to the battlements.

"I'll give you whatever you want," Winslow said. "And I'll divorce Ava, Stephanie. I've been planning to anyway."

"Really?" Stephanie asked. "Wouldn't it be better to kill her? Then you'd get—"

What Winslow would receive was never verbalized because Watson jumped and landed on Roger's face, digging his claws into the man's head and neck.

With a shout of pain, the professor staggered backward, releasing Ava's arm.

Watson leaped clear as Sean and Winslow tackled Roger and Stephanie. Faith guided Ava away from the brawl to safety.

In the tower room, Sean and Winslow tied the criminals to chairs.

Faith called the police again. "Is there any way to bump up our priority? We've got an attempted murder here."

21

"You think the porcelain figurine is in here?" Ava stood in the middle of Regina's bedroom and glanced around.

Ava had invited Faith and Brooke back to Wintersea. Faith couldn't believe her eyes when they'd passed through the gate earlier. Gone was the gloom that had pervaded the estate. Now the sun was shining, the gardens were blooming, and the grounds were bursting with color. Spring had arrived at last.

"That's what we figure," Faith said. "Somewhere she could keep an eye on it."

Brooke motioned to the stack of cardboard boxes near the door. "Winslow is letting you dismantle this place?"

Ava's eyes glowed with joy. "Finally. He admitted he'd been hanging on to Regina's things because he was so unsettled about her death. Something told his subconscious that she hadn't killed herself. And finding out that she had truly loved him seems to have allowed him to let her go." In an abstract movement, she smoothed her flowing top over her belly.

Could she be . . . ? Faith normally didn't make such comments, but she couldn't refrain. "Ava," she said teasingly, "do you have news for us?"

"What do you—?" The other woman glanced down at her midsection, where her hand still lingered. She laughed. "Yes, I do have news. We're having a baby."

Faith and Brooke launched into cries of congratulations and well wishes.

Brooke even gave Ava a hug and danced around the room with her, holding her hands.

"You two are so wonderful." Ava's eyes filled with tears. "I don't know what—"

Faith put up her hand. "Say no more. We're happy to help." She looked around the room. "Where do we begin?"

"Let's get the clothes packed first," Ava said. "That will get them out of the way."

In short order, they unloaded the closet and bureau drawers, folding the clothing to be donated to a charity. *Regina had good taste*, Faith thought as she loaded cashmere sweaters and designer trousers into a box.

"I heard the police figured out who your stalker was," Brooke said to Faith.

"They did. It was Tim Harrison. He wasn't involved with the blackmail, but he was worried I visited the shop to snoop into his business. He owes Wolfe money."

"I still can't believe Cassandra did that," Ava said softly. "You think you know a person . . ."

Cassandra had been charged with second-degree murder since she had pushed Valentina in anger but hadn't planned to kill her.

"And I'm still shocked about Roger and Stephanie," Brooke said.

They had been charged with first-degree murder of Regina Winterbourne as well as attempted murder of Ava. Roger had drugged Ava so that she missed her interview, slipping a sedative into the "soothing cup of tea" he'd given her to help her relax beforehand. He'd also drugged her so she wouldn't resist when he and Stephanie made their move to kill her.

Charges regarding Meg's fall were also pending. Stephanie had pushed Meg so she wouldn't notice Roger in the basement on his way back from the tower tunnel.

"Pride and greed," Ava said sadly. "The motives for much evil. That's why I'm donating the proceeds of my book to charity." Her smile was crooked. "And Regina's name is going to be in bigger print on the cover than mine. Much bigger."

Ava had discussed her book at the conference. In spite of its rough first night, the event had been a great success. One of the other speakers had filled in for Ava, who was then able to give her speech during his slot later, after she'd recovered from her ordeal.

Watson wove between their legs and entered the closet. He went to one side, where he sat looking up at the empty clothes rod.

"What is it, Watson?" Faith asked.

He didn't move.

Faith examined the wall more closely, knowing that Watson did nothing without purpose. She ran her fingers along the crack. It formed a rectangle. "What's this?"

Ava studied the line in the plaster. "That's the access panel for the plumbing. The bathtub is on the other side of this closet. See the screws?" She pointed.

Now Faith saw them. They weren't readily visible due to being painted over. "Are you thinking what I'm thinking, Brooke?" she asked. The panel was a perfect example of hiding something in a place that was so innocuous no one noticed it.

"Let me grab a screwdriver," Brooke said. "I remember seeing one in the kitchen."

She was back within a few minutes, and not long after that, they had the panel off the wall.

Ava looked down inside the cavity.

"Do you see anything?" Faith asked.

"I think so." Ava fished around. "There's something plastic down there." She pulled out a bundle and set it on the rug.

"Hurry, hurry." Brooke jiggled her knees like a little girl.

Faith and Ava shared an amused smile.

Ava ripped the plastic away to reveal a thick layer of packing wrap.

Brooke handed her a box cutter. "Thought we might need it."

With careful slicing and pulling, Ava revealed a gorgeous porcelain figurine in mint condition. With it was a packet of letters tied with faded ribbon. "Here, you open these." She handed the bundle to Faith, then placed the figurine on Regina's cleared desk by the window. It was the missing Meissen.

Faith slipped off the ribbon and divided the packet, passing half the letters to Brooke. Perching on the bed, they opened the envelopes. *Dearest Ralph*, read most of them. *My Gertrude*, read the others.

"We've got the love letters between Gertrude Lloyd and Ralph Briggs," Faith said. "No doubt they trace the story of their relationship."

"And exploits," Brooke said. "Listen to this. 'Once we obtain our nest egg, we can leave Cape Cod for Florida. I look forward to making a home with you among the palm trees and white sands.' That was Ralph."

The three women fell silent for a moment, their attention focused on the porcelain figurine. The sunshine picked out its fine details, gilding the Cupid's golden curls.

"I'll have to put it in a special place. A symbol of love." Ava rubbed her belly again. "Of love overcoming all obstacles. It's been quite a journey."

The cat jumped up beside his human, bestowing upon her the loud purr that signaled his approval. He rubbed his face on her hand. She patted him thoroughly, as he deserved.

Together they made a good team, but the truth was, she couldn't have done it without him.